Judge's Dreams

I

Juan Moisés de la Serna

Translator: Lina Jankauskaite

Published by Tektime

2020

Judge's Dreams I

Written by Juan Moisés de la Serna

Translator: Lina Jankauskaite

1st edition: August 2020

© Juan Moisés de la Serna, 2020

© Ediciones Tektime, 2020

Published by Tektime

https://www.traduzionelibri.it

No part of this book may be reproduced, stored in a retrieval system, or transmitted, in any form or by any means – electronic or mechanical, including photocopying, recording, or other means – without the prior written permission of the publisher. The infringement of these rights may constitute a crime against intellectual property (Art. 270, including the following articles, of the Penal Code).

Should a photocopy or a scanned copy of any fragment of this work be required, contact CEDRO (Centro Español de Derechos Reprográficos [eng. Spanish Centre of Reprographic Rights]). CEDRO can be contacted via website www.conlicencia.com or by telephone at 91 702 19 70 / 93 272 04 47.

Prologue

The judge fell asleep and, some three hours later, when he woke up rested and with his mind clear of the heaviness of the day, he established visual contact with a scene that he wasn't familiar with. As if he was transferred to some other place, where he could see and hear everything that was happening. The kind of presence, where he could observe all the assistants in detail, whilst not physically there.

It was the first time something like that has happened, and so he found himself with fear. In the beginning, he kept a distance from people that he was watching and events that he was witnessing. But soon, he realized that this could only be a dream, and nothing could really happen, and so he got mixing with the assistants, observing everything from different positions. When they did not detect his presence, he finally decided that, effectively, this was a dream, and that he could learn something from things that he was seeing and hearing.

Dedicated to my parents

Content

The First Dream

The judge fell asleep, and, some three hours later, when he woke up rested and with his mind clear of the heaviness of the day, he established visual contact with a scene that he was not familiar with. As if he was transferred to some other place, where he could see and hear everything that was happening. The kind of presence, where he could observe all the assistants in detail, while not physically there.

It was the first time something like that has happened, and so he found himself fearful. In the beginning, he kept a distance from the people that he was watching and events that he was witnessing. But soon, he realized that this could only be a dream, and nothing could really happen. So he got mixing with the assistants, observing everything from different locations of the room, and when they did not detect his presence, he finally decided that, effectively, this was a dream, and that he could learn something from things that he was seeing and hearing.

He had no idea how he found himself in a great hall, presided by the King himself. Someone who looked just like him was sitting beside the King. He was so surprised that he exclaimed out loud, 'What a strange dream! I see myself!' He knew that this reality was not physical, as well as that, in this dream, he continued being a judge. There were others just like him, also judges. As well as those who served as prosecution witnesses and those of the defense. There was also one who was presenting the case. He stated that the subject matter was the Elders of the Community. The one who seemed to be in charge, the current prosecutor, argued that they should be made to vanish, whilst the defense was saying that they were to be respected. And, in the end, he himself – or the one who looked like him – had to pass his JUDGEMENT, to state his opinion.

Once everything was over, the King, who was still present there – he was an observer, not a participant – made a decree upon this judgment. But all of this is better told in detail because it is important as the teachings then spread through some town.

For clarity, I must tell you here, in this first chapter, that the judge saw himself as a living being but, rather than made of physical matter, he was made of energy, which made him undetectable to others. But to himself, his senses were intact, and he could move from one place to another, not walking, like the physical body, but rather, thinking. Thoughts took him to where he wanted. It took a few attempts to learn to move this way because, usually, thinking bears no importance on the movement. So when what one thinks is suddenly fulfilled, one realizes the enormous capacity that a man has.

The judge, while the speech was taking place, moved from one place to another, passed between the characters, listening to their words and thoughts, finding many things out. He felt himself a part of that physical world but, at the same time, knew that it was all a dream. A dream that someone immensely powerful, someone Superior, has sent upon him. The very first thing he wanted to find out was who was it that sent him these moving pictures, and, to his amazement, he discovered that it was the HIGHEST himself.

This is what he saw. In a large rotunda-shaped room with pillars on the sides, some chairs along a large table were placed. There were five armchairs. It all looked like a tribunal hearing, where he himself was the judge. He arrived before the other people entered. He saw armed guards and understood that someone important – as he soon had confirmed – would be present. Well-dressed people began to come in, wearing what I would call luxurious cloaks and elegant hats covering their heads. And – as the case was – two characters that entered last, was the King, and another one, who looked like his Minister of Justice.

Those noble Lords sat down in their armchairs and

gave way for those of lesser rank to enter. As they were entering, they were saluting and bowing their heads right from the boor. To the judge's astonishment, he saw himself among that group.

Naturally, he realized that none of this was reality, for he was still asleep. But, at the same time, he was in this room as if he were a spirit; present, seeing, and listening.

They all took turns to stand and speak in front of the King. The following was said.

The King had summoned them as the best among those who considered themselves judges, and thus – although he was only a Capital Judge, without even his own jurisdiction, and could only administer justice in the souk – he was called because he had gained fame.

To publicly acknowledge the arriving at a judgment, they would say a prayer. They would say the right thing; thus, it would be a permanent truth. This is how all verdicts were usually recognized as fair; an aspect that, in other cases, did not prevail as the verdicts tended to favor one over another.

The unfair verdicts, the ones that tended to favor that who had better financial means, or stronger arguments, or that who had prepared better evidence, the rulings were given in their favor. The one who was inferior or ignorant never had justice served in their favor, therefore, among the people – and especially among the merchants – it was said that justice belonged to the powerful. Except for one judge. There was the one who always did the right thing.

The King had learned of this and wanted to check if what he was hearing was true, so he said to himself – against the advice of his Minister of Justice, who attempted to distract him from the matter, as it could cause them harm – that he wanted to witness this man passing a judgment. So, he presented himself disguised as an observer and, once he decided that he liked what he saw, he arranged Judgements to Society to be passed. It seemed that they now had a judge who came from the Justice of the Spiritual World, and people would benefit from it. After some thought, he arranged and called a tribunal, to be presided over by this very special judge.

When all had said their greetings and introduced themselves, the King sent the Minister of Justice to speak. He explained that he wanted to know how justice was served among the people, and that, to assess the competences of the judges, he had arranged for judgments to be passed before the King, who would listen but not intervene.

He said they did not want justice to be based on opinion but, instead, on the right thing to do. He also established who had to serve as the Accuser – or the Prosecutor – and who had to serve as the Defense. As well as who had to act as prosecution witnesses, and those of the defense alike. And, the last of all, he appointed the Chief Judge, who was none other than the dreaming judge.

The man, who struggled to shake off his amazement, who never liked being held important, and who, at this very moment, was sitting in the very last of all the chairs – the place considered the most remote and the least relevant – upon hearing his name called for the position, got up, and tried to excuse himself:

"I thank you for the position, but having those superiors to me here, and considering that I am the least of all those present, I think you have made a mistake in the appointment," the judge continued speaking slowly and in a voice for everyone to hear. The room was large. "Tell me, how are they, who are more, are now to be less, are to submit to my judgment? Is my word going to have any weight? Especially with the grand charges to be defended or prosecuted, and they are well prepared, while I hardly have what it takes to conduct justice in the souk. Which, as you know, are simple matters and do not require significant preparation."

He put his arguments forward and, just as the minister, who was in agreement with his explanation, was going to change things around, the King, who seemed to be the only one that was clearly determined to make it happen, intervened and said:

"Let us see how you do it, now that you are not in the souk, and how others handle being at your command rather than being those giving orders. Let the tribunal begin!"

Once this was settled, more chairs and tables were brought, and the tribunal was formed. Also, as the King wanted to keep a record – because he sensed that something important could come out of this – a court typist was called to put down on wax tablets what judgment will be passed, so that it can be either archived or applied, according to its value.

The judge – now that he was of such importance – asked for the subject matter that he will be required to rule on. He was advised on it and, rising to the power that the King himself awarded him, he ordered for the debate to be opened. But, as no one had the King's intentions communicated to them in advance, he arranged that they all have time until after lunch to think, to put their arguments together, and to prepare the witnesses.

All seemed happy with it, except for the King. He appeared to be in a hurry, as he said so himself.

The judge, acting as Judge, replied:

"See, my Lord, we can do as you wish, but if you want justice, this has to be well thought out as well as well-defended, and if someone, because they did not have the time they needed, does not do it well, then they will say that the King wanted it that way, that he did not want justice but speed instead."

The King understood and said:

"You are the Judge, you have the power. It will be done as you say."

The judge – the real one, the one who was sleeping in his bedroom at home – continued sleeping, while his spirit – the one that saw and heard everything and was still amazed at seeing himself in this surreal situation – was listening to all the commentary. He got closer to some of the important judges, without them noticing.

In fact, they were the most important among the judges, as well as considered to be significant men outside of courts too. Approaching, he listened to them murmuring that they would settle the score with the judge later, once they all left this place, while others said:

"We will let him do it, and, when time is right, we will set a trap for him in front of the King." They were all intelligent and enjoyed the support of the Minister of Justice, who clearly showed that he was not satisfied with the arrangement or with the roles assigned.

The judge – the one who had been given the position of the Judge by the minister following the orders of the King

– saw himself sitting alone on one side of the room and, when one of the other judges approached him, he heard himself say:

"Until the tribunal is over, I have nothing to comment. Your comments could also undermine the tribunal, knowing one side but not the other."

The chosen subject was THE ELDERLY. The hearing started once they had organized themselves. The Principal judge with the most authority began to speak. Since he was the one with the most authority, everyone was listening to him, and it was for everyone to see that he was trying to show off. But things that he was saying were nothing new. He had been told to present the case, and that is what he was doing. Without much detail, just to play his along.

Then the next one spoke, also Principal judge, second in authority, and everyone was listening to him. He made his presentations as an accuser – or the Prosecutor – and he himself realized, while on show, that he just wanted to get it over with and get out of there as soon as possible. He felt uncomfortable and considered this whole thing to be a King's whim.

Then came the third, the one who was appointed to serve as a Defender. Since the accusation had been put forward so badly, he did even worse, as he did not feel he could show up his superiors. And, although in the end, he tried to summarize and clarify what was said, it was apparent to everyone that he wanted to do the previous speaker a favor.

The prosecution witnesses and those of the defense continued, and so until the end. When everyone seemed to have finished, and the Judge's verdict was supposed to be passed – undoubtedly, it would be favorable to the principal of the highest authority, which everyone, including the King, expected, as it all seemed straight-forward – they found the Judge speaking the following:

"Let me go and say a prayer before you hear my Judgment," and he retired.

When he returned, his face indicated concern. And so, on his feet, he asked the King for permission to speak. The King granted it, and the judge said:

"Well, all of you now have had a chance to shine before the King, but if he wants justice, we will have to do things differently from how they have been done so far. Otherwise, we will continue to repeat the same mistakes that we have been making until now."

The principals took those words as an insult, and, rising from their seats, they started laying into the judge. But then, in turn, the King had begun to rise, calling them back loudly. And so they all fell silent again, and listened to him say:

"I am glad the Judge was the one to put you all in your place because, if he had not done it, I would have done so myself. The things I have seen are of no use to me, and I want things new and different. So stop worrying about looking good. To me, you are the Principals, and you do not stand to lose anything. So let the Judge do his job. Let's listen to what he has to tell us. Considering the length of time he spent preparing the speech, he must have more to say to us than he has so far." And he sat down.

With those words from the King, the judge felt his authority reinforced and began by organizing the work. He announced whom he wanted to hear first from and – as he had done before – said:

"I hope that you are better in your courts because today, you lacked quality. Prepare your work well for tomorrow." He did the same with all the others, surprising even the King who, on the one hand, at the beginning saw this to be a game, but, on the other hand, he liked the tone and the approach of him whom he appointed as a Judge. They all left discontented.

The Judge, resorting to the authority that the King had awarded him, ordered that the tribunal continued the following day. He spoke to each one separately and gave them time to prepare for their respective roles. Of course, with all that out in the open, and seeing that the King himself who until then ignored them was now taking part in the tribunal itself. Albeit only as a spectator, they all made an effort.

At this point, the Spirit of the Judge returned to his body, flying, making his own thought turn into reality. Before entering, he looked at the house from above and found it curious, as he had never seen the building from this angle. Upon entering the room, he saw his beloved wife sleeping peacefully. He found himself in another room, also sleeping, although in a rather unhealthy posture, and entered the body. When he did so, The Judge – the Physical Judge – woke up. He got up and went to his bed, feeling utterly exhausted.

The judge woke up the next morning and felt as if he was almost sleepwalking through his day as if he were not rested or had a fever. But he remembered every detail of what it was that he had to do. He remembered very well what he had dreamt. He felt so anxious that he decided to consult Him in Prayer. He was told:

"Await tonight for the dream is not over yet."

The day had eventually come to an end, too slowly for his liking. When the time came to get some rest, he fell asleep, totally exhausted. That, however, did not prevent him from waking up three hours later and reliving everything he had seen in the last night's dream. He then fell asleep again and re-entered the Court, where the ELDERLY was on trial.

The same thing as the night before happened. The Spirit of the Judge left the physical body and, after looking at it for just a moment, he thought of being in the King's palace. And just as he thought about it, he flew immediately over in the direction of the place where they had to meet up. He was the first to arrive, so he watched everyone else, the last of whom was the King, enter. The King sat down in his armchair, with the Minister of Justice as well as two more Ministers that he invited beside him. Once everyone was present, the Judge commanded to begin.

Tribunal began with the Judge explaining the reason for the gathering and setting out things that had to be done. He also brought up a subject of anyone potentially having any prejudices or pressures or motives for the tribunal to be deemed invalid. Everyone knew that to be the case, and so the Judge spoke aloud the words:

"I know that this is so; however, I understand that you are all Judges, so you should – before entering – be able to leave at the door whatever it may be that may affect what is said here."

All agreed, and it seemed that, with the night that they had to reflect, their aptitude had changed. They realized the Judge was being serious and could give them a cause to be concerned if they did not comply, especially with the King being there.

The Session was opened by him, who had to lay down the accusation and who you would call a Prosecutor. He argued that all the elderly at a certain age or of certain circumstances had to be either killed or permitted to die since they were now useless. Instead, they were a great burden to their family, who had to have people dedicated primarily to them. He argued that, in ancient times, when someone reached the moment of not providing any value anymore, they were left on the mountain to wait for their death, alone and starving. All there would be were two to four days of suffering. He said that it was nothing when compared with the years of suffering that they could otherwise endure if they were cared for, as it could last for years. And then there was suffering of others.

Everyone listened and, although they did not like the subject, it was well presented and well-argued. And so the man who seemed to be made of iron continued with his harsh words:

"Naturally, there are exceptions but, as a rule – and because a Judgment must encompass a general rule, and only then, in its light, each particular case is considered – I say that suffering neither purifies nor helps in your

Spiritual life. So there is no point in prolonging suffering because it is also worthless for your internal Spirit. After all, there the minds do not govern. And it is known that the Spirits and the physical body connect through the mind. So, if the mind does not work, this connection is interrupted. The Spirit is waiting for the death of the body to come, so it can leave it behind and go to a place where the Spirits dwell." Judging by the demeanors of the others, it seemed that what he was saying was considered right.

The Accuser – or the Prosecutor – called on one of his witnesses, who said that his father, whom he had lived with for a long time, was such a heavy burden that everyone wished for him to die. This had been going on for more than ten years. It was the consequence of an accident, a fall from a horse.

This was going on day in and day out. The man could hardly be moved because he was a heavy load and had problems with his back. He had to be bathed and his personal needs attended to. As you know, the sick do not have control of their functions, and thus he was often laying in filth. Everyone seemed to agree.

The man – who was a Judge of the assistants and who ended up with the role of a witness in support of the charge – was saying:

"I am the one who suffers the least since I hardly see

him. When I leave in the morning, he continues in his bed, and when I return, he is in his bedroom. All the work falls on the woman and the children, and they can no longer bear it, especially being aware that he occupies a space in the house which we need to be able to separate the children – who are both males and females. They are older now, but must continue sleeping together." He offered many arguments.

Once he was finished, the second prosecution witness continued:

"You will see that my case is different. I have a father who is already very old, and his mind is gone. But, since he is still alive, according to the Law, the inheritance cannot be distributed. So we just have to endure not being able to do anything while he says, 'Everything stays as it is. Once I am gone, you can sell up or do whatever else you want but, for now, all the assets are mine to do whatever I want with them.'"

"He does not believe that we would take better care of it if he left the money for us to manage. And he understands that, when he does not own the fortune anymore, we may abandon him or get rid of him, as has happened in some cases that he says to have known throughout his life. See, this is a lot for us to take; and his hair and beard are already grey. He constantly humiliates us by making us ask him for money to be able to continue with the estate. He is bad in the head, and he cannot look after it. He did not see that it was necessary to replace a pair of animals for mating in order to have good livestock. As you know, that costs a fortune. We told him, 'We sell a piece of land, and with the money we buy animals.' And, because he is not right in the head, he said to us, 'By the price you are telling me, it sounds like a robbery.'"

"Since he does not live in our times anymore, he thinks that everything is much cheaper. And there is nothing we can do."

The witness looked at everyone and, seeing faces reflecting agreement, continued:

"I end by saying that we want him to die, and we believe that things would be much better if such a thing would happen. In our case, he experiences no sufferings, but he has imposed the suffering on us. He seems to have still a body that can endure life, and it will mean ruin to all us brothers." And here he closed the matter.

The Judge listened, but his face was not giving away whether he was convinced or not. Everyone knew that a judge could not show whether he agrees with any of the parties and that he must reserve that for when the passing of the Judgment comes. Regardless, everyone still expected to glimpse some indication. The prosecution witness finished his presentation, but he spoke again and said:

„I reserve the right to speak again, in the end, after the Defence has spoken." And, although this kind of thing was rarely ever done, he wanted to show off in front of the King and had thought of this as something unusual to impress him.

The accuser – or prosecutor – finished, and gave the floor to the Defender, who proceeded with the following:

"When a person is sick, they are cared for, so life can go on. If, when we are of no use, when our minds are not bright – because of fever or illness – they look after us, life can continue. This kind of situation can often last quite some time, sometimes even longer than a year, but once it has passed, it is forgotten. How can we treat the elderly as a disease?"

"We are all bound by ties of brotherhood and consider that we have a Spirit within. We are not animals. We have humility, as well as feelings and obligation to help those who need us. That is the basis of our Communities. Look at that – since ancient times – our communities have been formed on the basis of MUTUAL HELP AND MUTUAL PROTECTION."

The Defender, looking around at everyone and seeing from the faces that his arguments were well-conducted, continued.

"But, what is more, we have been taught since ancient times, and we know it from tradition, and also from some writings, that customs as barbaric as those that have been just presented justifying these deaths, were disavowed by the Spiritual Masters. We have been told that our actions have a spiritual undercurrent. To think, what would that make us if, not only we do not look after those who need and try to make their death easier for them, but, instead, leave those people to die without assistance?"

"Looking at us as representatives of everyone," continued the Defender arguing," we are all of the age that we will soon be considered to be elderly. And age will also happen to our children, as time passes. We are imposing harm on these people for having the disease of old age. And, above all, we promote the lack of comprehension in the youngest, for which we ourselves will be judged when the time comes."

"We will be committing a crime. The greatest crime that can be committed. They are defenseless beings, and they need our help. They have been giving themselves to others throughout their lives. For this reason, I say and maintain that the elderly must be respected and treated with the courtesy and affection they deserve as people. As well as parents of those who now want to get rid of them and take what is theirs."

"But not only this. Right now, you are trying to decide whether it is right or fair to support the elderly who are of no use to humanity while they are alive. Keep in mind that, if we are not going to offer arguments to some powerful or not so powerful as to how to stop all those relatives imposing their will, then they will have the right to decide for themselves."

"See that, based on the above, they will only stay with those who they know will treat them right. We will be covering a crime with the corresponding actions of that who will become the victim. And, as you know, that who is in danger of death has all the right to the Defence."

"But also consider that, if we do such a thing, all those who reach a certain age will have made sure that their fortunes had been exhausted. And they will not worry themselves with securing their estates, so as to ensure that nothing is left to that who would execute them in order to keep their property when the supposed time comes."

"You know that everyone who owns something is concerned that their assets be preserved through others. As well as that, although some may think that hoarding assets here on Earth is foolish, some people feel like that, and the Kingdom is an excellent example of it." As soon as the Judge said this, he realized that he had just meddled with the Crown, which was a mistake. And so he continued to correct himself. ”Not to say that this latter case is a bad example but, rather, the desire to ensure the best of everything for their own, so all can live in better health and with access to food and clothing for all.” And, when he considered that he has recovered from the failure, he continued. ”Of course, the matter that we are deciding on is important! But what also lays behind it, is the fundamental question of, ‘Who has the right to give themselves permission to kill?’ Because that would be what all men would think as they gradually approached old age. Or who has the right to kill another? Because would it not be – and that serves to reflect – the father who had that right over his children who, after all, have come from him?”

”Perhaps when I wished I would not have that right?” The Defender continued. ”And then, if we deny it to him, how can we give that right to the children, if the father is that who has given them life? Or, maybe, men of our minds do things that defy nature?”

Here he made another mistake and, after immediately realizing that, corrected himself again.

”Admittedly, nature has these customs developed in some animals. But if we carry out such act, we become carnivore animals, who kill to be left with the resources of others or simply because they do not benefit us, even when they do not bother us.”

Here, the Defender paused, and utilized what in the trials is known as "the silence of attention." By allowing for this silence, one has everyone still, waiting for what follows, and focusing attention on the next thing that is going to be said. The Defender, raising his voice, continued:

"So I raise my voice, as loud as I can, to say that life is important and no one has the right to take it! And if one has fought for their Country, for their land, for their family, no one from this Country, from these lands, or from his family has any other right than to protect them until the end of their days."

After that, it was the turn of a Defense witness who said:

"You know me as a Judge, and you also know my reputation that I never lie. I want you to listen to this story, which is real and was not only prepared for this defense."

"I have my father in my home, and I feel blessed having him beside me because he is a wise and just man, and he brings his wisdom into the house. He can hardly help out at home, but what he gives is a pleasant compensation of joy and sweetness. It has been five years that he is with us and, although we hope that he will heal, we do not know. He was in an accident where he was run over by a soldier's mount, which left his back with injuries, and his legs suffered several fractures. We know that he will never be the same and that he will always need help, but his head is just fine, and he continues teaching his wisdom to everyone around him."

"I also want to emphasize that he is very close to my children, whom he loves more than he loved us, and it shows that they match it back in the same measure. One of my daughters says that she wants to take him home with her. She is getting married soon, and he would provide company and sound advice, which they will need for they are young."

The witness had his say and, when he had nothing more to add, he finished up assuring that his father was a very different person before. He had always been busy with work and merchandise; he was a merchant who had little time for his family.

"But, since the accident, what we lacked before he is now giving us and, although it was a disgrace that we hope he will heal from, I bless the moment of the accident for the change we have had in him."

Then it was the turn of the Judge who was acting as a second witness of Defense. After he greeted everyone, he went on to say what he had prepared:

"I do not have a personal testimony to offer, but that of many men and women who would have to change their ways of thinking if we were to do something as monstrous as authorizing the death sentence for the elderly. And that is what our accusing judge – or prosecutor – has tried to convince us to do."

"As you will know, a long time ago, Druids arrived in these lands and settled. We derive from them in terms of our culture and our ways of thinking. And, although some of our concepts differ now, such as the Spiritual. As you know, for the Druids, nothing existed after life, but everything returned to mother earth or nature. We believe that there is a spiritual life after the physical one and that it is lived in the form of Spirit, the Spirit that we all carry within ourselves. But our differences are not in terms of physical life."

"We know, and we are taught in the Spiritual School as children, that the Spiritual world exists, and that everyone who has been good in the physical world will be allowed in. Apart from those who have committed a crime against life. The principle that we are taught, the one of the twelve, is that Life is sacred."

"The principles on which our customs and our traditions are based are basic – RESPECT FOR LIFE AND HELP another when they are in need. These two fundamental pillars are not only Spiritual. When we entertain this idea of killing or letting die, we forever lose our right to preach the Upper world."

"See, what we are here discussing is the killing of the very special people to whom the Society – as well as families and communities – owe a lot. Or letting them die. For that reason, I fear that we may be authorizing something that others do not want and do not think to accept."

"Will the Judge who will be passing this Judgment please consider that he may have to get soldiers to carry it out? And let him consider the communities of the mountains. None of them will comply. Or the communities of the valleys, and of the lowlands, where the commitment to unity is even stronger. How can we, a few judges, even with a King in front of us, claim the right to try to change something so deeply rooted in our own Ethiopian essence?"

The man was radiant, and he knew he was heard. He was good at reading the public, so he did not prolong the subject so as not to spoil it. He ended with:

"So I tell you, if you approve of such a thing, you will not be worthy of being Ethiopian."

And, as a man who had put forward his argument in this manner, he took a few minutes of silence so that his last statement can settle in everyone's mind. After confirming that it was over and saluting everyone, he sat down.

Now, everyone was watching the Judge, who got up to

speak in front of the King. He greeted him and said:

"As you can see, my Lord, it has gotten late. If you wish, we will continue later because the morning is over, and the noises in the guts of the attendees could be heard for quite some time now." At that, everyone smiled because it was true. The King himself had noticed it and said:

"Very well, we shall continue later. But, remember, you cannot take the discussions of this subject outside with you, because you have the whole city listening and that would not serve justice." He got up and left the chambers.

When they resumed the session, the King, who had been waiting for the right moment, said:

"So, now is the time when you say your prayer and ask for advice before you pass your judgment, right?" He was looking at the judge who, in turn, replied:

"See, my Lord, Justice cannot be done a hurry. Remember that the Accuser – or the Prosecutor – had reserved the last turn, after the Defense had spoken. So it is now up to him to continue."

The Judge to whom he had referred took the floor. However, he came short. He had initially intended to make a great speech, but the apparent haste that the King had shown advised him against it. He determined that he had nothing new to add, and so the time for Judgment to be passed had come.

The judge, the Spiritual Body, observed himself serving as a Judge's in a court session that was all a dream. He saw himself take the floor and say:

"You will have seen, my Lord, how the matter has been presented. It is not an easy task. As a Rural Judge, I have not been gifted with wisdom."

"Remember that I only administer Justice in the Souk and for the Souk, so I need all the help that can be given to me. That is why I always retire – to ask for it. I do it through Prayer. You all know that, when we do that, our Spirit gets connected to the Spiritual Master, which is always attending to us, young men."

"You also know that this Master – who to me is SUPREME – is the one who always advises. In my case, he always does so in all aspects of life, in which I feel that I want to consult him. He advises me in the courts and tells me what I have to say. All I do is repeat in words the ideas that he had given me."

As the King – attending in disguise – had seen him conduct the tribunal, he did not believe that the advice that this man can receive could give him any greater wisdom than he himself had so, upon hearing this, he jokingly said:

"Go and ask for this advice, and make sure that it is a good one. And that it is different from the one we all know. If not, we may find that it is your own mind that advises you, and what you are looking for in the Prayer is time to think as you are already old."

The judge considered this to be an insult and blushed. He turned to the King and said:

"My Lord, you have the strength, but not the reason. If the reason is sustained by force when you are deciding what you expect from your people, you will be hated rather than loved. Because, if justice is done under pressure and by force, no other but fear will result. Is this what you are seeking?"

Everyone was suddenly frightened by the words he had addressed towards the King. Even the Judge himself. Therefore, he assumed an attitude of submission that would please the King and said:

"I think your comment is good and fair, albeit a little harsh. I want my people not to fear me. So take the time you deem appropriate, and we will see if that advice is worth the time that we are losing."

The judge – the Spirit – watched how the Judge retired from the court hall and into a solitary place where he began to pray. After some time, he saw the sloping figure nod and nod again. It continued for some time; he sat down on his heels, and with his eyes closed, he listened. When he had finished, he left the room and went back out to where everyone was waiting. The King said:

"It is late, so, as you need your time, we will continue tomorrow. Everyone, go now, and return for the second session." And that was when everyone knew that it was time for the sun to become vertical.

In the morning, everyone gathered again. The Judge greeted the King and the Minister of Justice first, followed by the other ministers who had come. There were already several others in addition to those that were invited by the King. They have heard about this and, not wanting to be left in the dark, they came of their own initiative. He greeted his companions and proceeded to speak.

"You see, my Lord," he addressed the King." The one who listens to me and the one who advises me has also listened to your words, and said the following:

'Tell your King that he can cut off your head as he has that power; that he can cut off your tongue as he has that power; and that he can sell you for a slave to the Egyptians because he has that power too. But the voice of the Spirit cannot be silenced. If he does not speak through my lips today, he will do it through someone else's. Because, if the Spirit must manifest itself, the power of the King is not enough to stop it. You see, if he so wanted, he could choose your own lips to speak to others.'"

Everyone found themselves frightened because they knew about the power of the Spirits. They understood that the Spirit of that man had to be very powerful to explain what he did. Right there, in front of him, was the one who was in charge of the Temple – or of the Spiritual School. Upon hearing these words, he became scared and approached the King to tell him something in private. The King was looking serious and said nothing until The Judge finished. Then the King spoke up and said:

"See, all this is new to me. I never wanted to offend anyone, neither Spirit nor my citizens. And you yourself are respected, since you are old, and I have given you the role of a Judge. So, continue with the subject matter and let us end this."

And here, the judge began to explain what he had been told.

"You see, a man has two bodies: one is Spiritual, and the other is physical. We all know very well that we see with the physical body and suffer from it too. But, if we look, neither of the two bodies had been made by us. Therefore, I am asking now – who made these bodies? The parents made the physical. But what about the Spiritual? Who is he, with a disposition of the physical world, to condemn the body which the Spiritual world inhabits? Do we not carry the obligation to protect our body from suffering for the Spiritual one to find rest in?"

The judge posed more questions, some of which seemed

to be intended to help, and others to condemn. He continued:

"The Judgment is as follows, and it will depend on the scenarios that I am going to discuss. If the children or people who are in charge of the elderly have benefited from the elderly person's resources, which they acquired during their life, they should welcome them with love and readiness. If this were not the case, or if they had been mistreated, the Authority would remove the elderly. It would also remove their assets and give them to someone who wanted to host them."

"If the old man has no assets, neither the children nor relatives are obligated to look after him. But if he raised someone or contributed towards someone with what he generated throughout his life, in the name of Justice, that, who had received these benefits, will be the one who has to return it, when the need arises. This includes the Kingdom that gets the taxes from its people."

"See, there may be many different circumstances, but I will only refer to three. The first being that which I just laid out. The second is the one where one has children, but they do not want him. Because he is a hindrance, or they want to kill him because he occupies space in the house, or because his mind is not what it used to be. In those cases, the King, in the name of Justice, with the help of the judges, should intervene. The situation will be heard and remedied."

"All citizens will be able to go to court and ask for justice when they feel harmed. And when they do not have resources, Justice will be free. As for those who make a living from justice, they collect the taxes. So, if they need or want justice, they will have to pay for it, as it cannot be charged to the Kingdom by a request of a wealthy individual."

"If a Judge hears a case of an old man who is not wanted at home – or if he incidentally finds out by himself of an old man who is being mistreated – he will visit him, talk to him, and will always hear him out. He will also listen to the family because the elderly can also sometimes not be in their right mind. It is, indeed, the reality that they can become strange and selfish."

"But if he sees that it is true and that it is the children who do not want him by their side and who mistreat him or want to kill him, the Judge will determine that he is better off being cared for elsewhere, by a family that wants him. The costs of his care and maintenance will be borne by the children."

"The children might not have received any assets, but they do not seem to know to pay back the life they were provided with by the old man. They do not know what it took from the old man when they were children. The sleepless nights, the care it took when they were both healthy and when they were sick. And, sometimes, the protection. Without ever thinking once that, one day, when he needed it, it will have to be paid back to him."

"But there is also the third scenario, you see. And that is the responsibility of the Kingdom to those who have been paying their taxes throughout their lives. So now that they need assistance, and nobody wants to help them, the King, as Lord of Justice, has to intervene and help the one who has been helping him his whole life."

"For this reason, a system should be formed, which would create places where they would be accommodated and looked after with kindness. These unique places should be built thinking of them and the difficulties they face, and good food, as well as good clothes, should be provided."

"The meeting of the needs that the elderly person has, such as food, hygiene, and medicines, as well as other things, must be guaranteed. And those who will care for these elders, the specially dedicated people, will also have to be remunerated and required to do their job well."

"This will have to be paid by the Communities because they had also benefited from that helpless old man's work, their love, as well as their help when it had been necessary. When a fire occurs or when heavy rains arrive, or when The

Communities are attacked by gangs of assassins, who defend them? The soldiers, yes, but they are not enough. Those who live in the Community contributes. So the Community is in DEBT."

"So that this does not serve as a surcharge to taxes, it would only be fair that, when someone receives an inheritance from their elders, they contribute to the Community a third of the inheritance. This is to cover the expenses of those who have nothing. After all, those who receive it have done nothing themselves to have earned that wealth. It had been given to them. So let that gift also to be distributed among those who have nothing."

"And it needs to be ensured that it will not be surrendered to someone in particular but, instead, given to the King. He will ensure that money is always available to cover the needs of all those who have lived under his rule. Thus, he will be in charge of collecting this part of the inheritances from those who receive it. Everything will be paid to the King, and the King will give it back to the Community, which will be responsible for the wellbeing of its people."

"Thirdly, if someone hasn't contributed anything that they would have to be paid back for – because they were foreign or because all their life they did not receive a salary and, hence, nothing was paid to anyone, which in itself is something very strange since it could be seen as if the collection does not work, but it is well known that it does – the Kingdom will be the one who has to pay and assume as a debt what the old man had spent. He has been in his land before he turned old, and he has been eating and spending, and with it, he has negotiated his right, and the owners of the land have allowed it."

"It creates an obligation in the same way as when one allows someone to enter their home. And, if this results in expenses or losses, one must assume it because he allowed them to come in. If one did not want to assume the responsibility, one should not have let them in." The judge continued. "Now, I will announce the final Judgement. And since we are all going to end up in those kinds of situations sooner or later – if we do not disincarnate before – it is better that we build these places where the elderly can be looked after."

"This will be especially suited for all the Capitals and large cities, where the number of people is considerably high, and where there will be many similar cases. It is not very common in rural Communities, where the elderly are respected and cared for in a particular way, where their wisdom is considered to be helpful to all."

"There will have to be a farm where no rent needs to be paid. Not too close as to not be disturbed, but not too far either so that everyone can come to parties and celebrations and take part in everyone's joyful occasions. As well as have dedicated places for celebrations built in these farms."

"These places have to be planned giving regard not to someone's taste and the foreseen duration, but to those who are going to be using them. These buildings will be adequate and made of suitable materials, both outside and inside, keeping in mind the cold weather, which can affect the elderly so much. Good food will be served there. And they will be given the help of employees, who will be more responsible than family members. That way, they can be calm about the future and can see life as worth living. And so the following should be considered:

'First, it is important that the house where they will live is at a ground level, at the height of a man so that the energies that are just above the ground do not affect them.'

'Second, the construction will be made of wood. It will not only have to be good and durable on the outside but also the inside. Both the floors and the walls will be double, and in between will be filled with clay, from which potters make goldsmiths. It is a good insulator for both winter and summer temperatures, and unwanted bugs do not nest inside.'

'Third, the roof will have to be built in two slopes. But

it will not be oriented as it is done now, which, as you all know, is facing the sunrise. In this case, you will change it to put a wall on the side where the sun rises, and the other one where the sun sets. The door will be facing the south, where the star of your forefathers appears.'

'I believe – and I am finishing – that the elderly should be treated as persons, with all the respect that our elders deserve. They must be taken care of with the same dedication that they would give to others, giving them what it is that they need. And, if they cannot be cared for by their own relatives, someone will have to be entrusted with it. And the elderly will not incur any cost liabilities.'

'For all of these reasons, if any elderly person does not have a family, the care will have to be provided at the expense of the Kingdom, to which we all contribute our taxes. It will care for these people until the end of their days, and it will do it with the same level of dedication as if it were his family. If there are complaints or it emerges that there are losses of funds for the enrichment of others, from the private fortunes of those responsible, he will get double the amount that he was cheated out of. And then the same again to make sure that they do not do it again in the future.'

'But there is still one last thing left, for this will be important in all the Capitals and the cities. There will have to be Judges who will be in charge of making all this work well. The reason why I say Judges is because they know how to balance Justice, and they know that listening to one side will not cut it and that both sides need to be heard, seen, and tested, if necessary. Community Authorities are not prepared for this, nor do they have the right people.'

"See, my Lord," he addressed the King. "If this worked well, all of those who are now nearing to those aging moments and who feel frightened by it, would thank you and send you blessings. And you," and he motioned towards the Ministers, "You are also subject to this because, right now, none of you can know what a son will do when it comes down to it."

Having said this, the Judge fell silent and looked at the King, who was sitting with a thoughtful gaze. Looking around at everyone, the King said:

"I have enjoyed bearing witness to this Tribunal. It was a good idea to hold it. I want the Judgment to be taken note of because I will want it to be put into practice. I now have you by my side as friends, and I also want to have you as friends when our heads turn white." And, addressing the Minister of Justice, the King said to him, "I congratulate you for what has been said here. In truth, they are judges of great value. It is my opinion that, what had been passed here as a judgment, is to be made known and to be stated in Law."

The King got up and left. The others, too, got up and left with him. Although not all of them. The one who ran the Temple and oversaw the Spiritual School approached the judge to talk to him in private.

The others also wanted to congratulate him, so they were waiting for their turn while the one who ran the Temple was speaking to the judge. And while they waited, they heard him say:

"The truth is, judge, we already know each other, just in a different way. You are a very special man, and you have the Master of the Masters for a Spirit that is watching over you. This wisdom that you have demonstrated here cannot come from anywhere else but Him. Come see me someday, and we will have to take as long as need be. I am in need of your advice."

Those who were listening were amazed because they knew this man. They knew that he was considered very strong and hard and, thus, his ways of dealing with others were not the most courteous. Hearing him talk in such a humble way astonished them, as well as the response that The Judge gave to him:

"Do not worry. Your questions will soon be answered, right here in this same place." The other man looked at him, lowered his head, and left.

After a moment of silence, they went ahead to congratulate the Judge on his Judgment, which had been just and clear. In the meantime, the King returned and said to them:

"I will be summoning you again, and next time the subject will be JUSTICE." And he left.

Everyone was surprised and suddenly felt frightened, for it could affect all of them. Several began to speak at the same time, one over another, not listening to each other. The King returned again – he did not seem too eager to leave – and said:

"And the presiding Judge will be the same. You can change the roles of others if you wish." He turned to his minister, who had returned with him, and said, "Take charge of it."

The Spirit judge returned to where the real one – the physical one – slept and re-entered him. In truth, it all had taken a long time. Both the Spirit and the physical body were exhausted from all the effort. He woke up remembering everything that took place and laid back down on his bed to get some sleep, for he desperately needed to rest.

His wife had seen him get up and return to bed and let him sleep until he woke up by himself, which turned out to be mid-afternoon. Once he had cleared his head with the help of bathwater, and with a good meal, he remembered everything again. They prayed. He then told a part of it to his wife, who said:

"Write down everything that happened in the DREAM, so that nothing is lost. And then rest because you have deserved it. You will come to have another DREAM, but not until you are fully rested."

Judge's Dreams I

The Second Dream

A few days after having finished writing up the whole of the Tribunal that he had seen in the DREAM and having revised it so that nothing had been forgotten, The judge, the Servant of the HIGHEST, was notified that he would have another Dream. This time the subject would be Justice and, since Justice was the most important thing of all, the Judge hoped that there would not be any failures and that it would be started soon. The Dream was to be special.

The lesson to be learned on this subject was, undoubtedly, of great importance, since the King's own Authority as the Supreme Judge of the Kingdom was in doubt. The event unraveled as follows.

It just so happened that the King had died in strange circumstances. The one who wished to proclaim himself the new King sent for the Minister of Justice and two more Judges from the Capital to confirm the identification of his father's body and to attest in accordance to the Law that the successor had nothing to do with the death of the previous one.

For a long time, it had been known that the late King's son was ambitious and wanted to wage wars on other nations. He was never satisfied with what he had, and he was overwhelmed with a young man's ambition, which made him undertake ventures that served him but wronged for others.

One of the judges that were called was the oldest judge, and, because of that, the others regarded him highly. In those lands – at that time – the elderly were greatly respected for the wisdom that they had accumulated within them.

When the judge was called to visit the King's residence, he was not told the reason for the call. He was surprised to be notified by the Minister of Justice himself, for they did not get along very well. The latter always strived to look good in front of the King regardless of any cost to others.

Upon presenting himself at the King's residence, he was received by soldiers and taken to the place where the meetings were held, to stand before one of the King's sons. The Minister and another Capital Judge were already here, so he presented himself, said "Hello," and approached the man with the most authority in the room – the Minister – to asked for the reason for this call. He was told:

"The King is dead. We are required to attest to his death and that his heir had had nothing to do with it. This is the Law, and it has to be handled in this way."

The judge was upset by the loss of the King because, even though he had not done much for the people, he had ensured that there were no wars and that everyone had a common understanding, especially regarding the other two neighboring Kingdoms. Since he had never been required to perform such a procedure before, he asked what the reason that he was picked to be called upon was. He was told:

"You are the oldest." And everything became clear.

They entered the room where the King was laid on a bed, and they all passed by looking at him. The Judges and the doctors that were also present checked his hands and his feet as well as his tongue and pronounced the King dead. When the old judge's turn came, instead of approaching the King, he retired to a discreet place in the back of the room to say a Prayer. Those who saw him do that thought:

"He is old. Look, he chose this kind of moment for prayer."

Once finished, the judge approached the group that was waiting for him and said:

"I want to see the King." Everyone who had already seen the King, let him pass.

He looked at him and asked for a needle. He proceeded to make three punctures to the King's body; first, in the forehead – and normal blood came out; second, in one of the arms – and blood came out; and last, in one of the King's feet – and blood came out again. He asked the doctors:

"How is it possible that the blood comes out if he died yesterday?" And he affirmed. "This man is still alive; the body is alive."

Everyone was astonished. The doctors approached again to look at the King. They picked up a polished piece of metal and put it under King's nose. As the metal did not steam up, they said:

"He is dead."

To which the judge replied:

"I believe not. You are mistaken."

At this point, the son stood in front of his father and, with viciousness or rage, using his fist, gave him a significant blow to his chest. He then roared at them:

"Who can take such a blow and not move?" And, looking at the judge, he said, "Attest or march on so that another can be sought."

At that moment, the judge replied:

"I will not attest, nor will I leave because the King is alive." At that moment, the son felt the King's hand on his arm.

The son, frightened, ran away, and the doctors and Judges approached their King as he recovered from what seemed like an assault. It was later discovered that poison had been put in his wine glass. But the discovery of who had done it or how it was done has nothing to do with the Dream that I am about to tell you about.

When the judge returned home to his wife from this gloomy experience that he had been called out to without being foretold for what reason – and he returned carrying the knowledge that his King had been poisoned by his own son, which was sad – she consoled him. He took a very hot bath, his wife fed him a nice creamy sweet and sour vegetable soup, which is the best for toning the body, and went to bed.

One day, while in his house, the judge sensed that that night he was going to have a new vision, so he prepared himself. He knew from whom the message was coming, so he prayed in an even more profound and prolonged way so that his Spirit can prepare for the job being sent to him.

Several days had passed since that day. One midnight, he suddenly felt a great uneasiness and understood that he was wanted to be spoken to. He woke up, sat up, then got up, and began to pray. He was told the following by the HIGHEST:

"Faithful servant, wake yourself up with cold water and listen to what I have to tell you because you are soon going to DREAM again."

The judge did everything he had been told to do and settled in an armchair. He waited, and in that wait, he found himself transposed while still being aware of everything. He observed his physical body sleep, and then as if nothing happened, he left through the roof of the house and flew towards the place where the King resided.

He entered the same hall where the first tribunal had been held. He inspected the entire room and, seeing that it had six windows, he said to himself, "That is a bad number, there should be seven," as it was considered that number seven was the luckiest. He continued thinking to himself, "And the throne should be in front of the odd window."

He observed that there were two exits, one of which was an emergency exit. It was disguised as if it were a wall; one could not distinguish it. However, when he put his foot against a particular part, the wall turned, and he discovered a staircase that was covered by a large curtain. He inspected – in detail – the King's armchair and found that, at the bottom of it, a sword was attached. It was put in a way that made it easy to remove it. He was taken aback by all the precautions but still thought that the King had not had all the securities in place.

Shortly after arriving there, he saw others begin to enter. First, some came in, then came the one who was himself – a man that looked very much like him – and who defended Justice by holding the position of the Judge. Finally, the King and his two great ministers – one of them of Justice, and another King's invitee – entered.

He saw the King instinctively stoop down and feel the hilt of the sword with his hand. Then, the Tribunal began.

The King took the floor and ordered the Tribunal to begin. But then the one who was the Minister of Justice took the floor and asked the Judge to change the subject for the Tribunal to be deciding on, for they were all judges, and they may feel uneasy about the potential outcomes. He said:

"See, my Lord, as well as we could never hold a Tribunal to pass Judgment regarding the crown or its privileges, the same applies to the subject of Justice."

With these words, the Minister of Justice thought to have presented the matter well, but the King, who was brave, took it up and said:

"The King's will must be obeyed. Otherwise, it may cause harm to third parties. And I do not see why that should happen. As the third party is the Judges themselves, they will endeavor to ensure that this does not occur. Come to think of it, it is almost like a Tribunal of intelligence itself, since they have to play their part, but they also have to be careful depending on the role they draw." The King paused to check that everyone understood that he would not back down and continued. "And you will see that the Tribunal will be testing that who serves as a

Judge the most, for he will be the one who has the last word. And, as I see that you are interested in knowing the subject for the next Tribunal, I can tell you that it will be the RULERS."

Everyone's roles were assigned, and the Commander of them all, the Minister of Justice, approached the one who was acting as a Judge – none other than the judge that was dreaming – and said:

"I hope that you will think well of everything before you speak, lest you end up harming the third parties, and, as a result of the King's game, the Justice of this country will come to be ruined."

The judge looked at him but did not answer. However, the King had seen the minister speak to the judge, and said:

"Come and tell me what it is that you said to the one who is presiding as a judge, for you seem to be uneasy about the outcome."

The minister stepped forward and for all to hear, including the judge, said:

"My Lord, I have advised him to be prudent and courteous, and to think hard about everything, because, from Tribunals as high as those which the King himself presides over, a change can come. And so it is important."

The King seemed satisfied, although he was not

entirely convinced that those were the words that were spoken. But, since he did not want to offend his minister, he said:

"Don't worry. If something that does not serve comes out of this, you are my advisor, you just tell me, and I will change it." Everyone sighed with relief.

The one who was opening the case and who was also a Judge, just like the rest of them, was about to start the matter when the judge that was assigned to preside over the Tribunal jumped ahead and said:

"As today's Tribunal is unique because we are playing ourselves, I want to suggest a modification. Let us consider that we are judging a case in which a man claims Justice against the injustice of a Judge. Let us say that a rural Judge like I have been for so long, has to hear the one prejudiced by injustice, and initiate a Tribunal for it to be decided. He has to go to a Capital Judge to have injustice rectified, and Justice served if you like," he looked at the King. "We can approach it in this way." Everyone agreed, for they were familiar with those kinds of cases.

The King seemed satisfied with it, and the Tribunal began. It was opened by the Judge in charge of presenting the case, who started by saying:

"As there had been no time to prepare, please excuse me for how little I have to say, for what I know of the case is as much as the Judge has just said."

After saying that, he ended his presentation. Everyone seemed satisfied; everyone but the Judge, as will be seen later.

The Accuser – or the Prosecutor – saw that this was easier than he had thought before it started and relaxed. He made a compelling presentation by saying that the rural judge did not have enough experience and that the Justice had to be mindful of his lack of training. Meanwhile, the people who go to Tribunal to challenge a Judgment made by a wiser Judge – that of the Capital – did not have to be heard. So if they raised a case for the rural Judge hear, they had to be fined for the damages it could cause.

The matter was simple. There had been a dispute over some land. One side said that he had bought it and paid for it and that from that moment it belonged to him. The other side agreed but, as seeds were planted in that land before the sale, argued that everything they harvested was not a part of the deal. And that this began to provide from the end of the harvest and that the harvest ended.

The person who was making a claim and who already had a court Judgment against him was the one who had bought the land. He wanted to keep what had been sown previously for, obviously, it carried value. He argued before the rural judge that, when he bought the land, no one had said to him that he could not keep what was already sown there. The way that he saw it was that it was in his interest that the first harvest had already been planted when he bought the land and that this harvest will be the beginning of the return.

The rural Judge, who should have been well acquainted with the subject of the land, the customs, and the ways of making various deals, understood that the buyer was right, and so he passed the Judgment in his favor. But all this had already been decided by a Capital Judge, where the one who sold the land had settled and where he had gone to make a claim.

The case that had been presented was real; everyone knew of it. Everyone understood that the Judge had chosen this case to get himself out of the problem of having to pass Judgment on Justice. Since they did not want this to proceed either, they decided to all be helpful so that they can finish the day well and leave there in peace.

The case had been presented to a Judge of a Capital who did not travel to inspect the land in question. Nor did he take a statement from the other party. Instead, he had been guided by the numbers and invoices that had been presented to him as the claim was made once the huge harvest had already been collected and sold knowing the price of it.

It had also emerged that the person who had collected the harvest had been the land's former owner. He had done so against the will of its current owner, turning up on the land with the hired day laborers and the buyers of the harvest, from where they had directly collected it and took it away, leaving only stubble on the land and nothing else.

To finalize it and to ensure that everything was legal, the one who had acted like this had taken out a claim against the one who had bought the land – but did not get to harvest anything – and obtained a favorable Judgment to end everything.

The prosecutor presented the arguments that were convenient to him, to make seem reasonable the person who had made a claim in the Capital and, effectively, against the judgment of the rural judge, whom he accused of not knowing the laws, as well as of possible acquaintanceship with the buyer. He also hinted that there was a possibility that, as a judge, he had been the one who had put the idea in the land buyer's head to make a claim against the buyer of the harvest.

As everything was very clear in this Tribunal, the prosecution witnesses were not called; instead, it was stated that they had witnessed the sale and that it had been legal, as well as the first Tribunal, which had also been just.

When the Defender's turn came, he praised the dedication and honesty of the rural judge and, although he did admit that the rural judges had little training, he continued to say that it was the only justice that could be had at that time with the meager means that were available as rural judges were not paid but only got what they made from the Trials.

He argued that the importance of Justice is unique, given that it represented the King himself. And that, if soldiers are essential in the event of a conflict, in peacetime, what mattered was Justice. If it functions well, everyone is happy, but if it fails, the King himself fails. Upon saying this, he realized that this last phrase had been ill-picked, and he changed his stance, having taken into account the presence of the one whom he just exposed.

The Defender argued for a long time, and it became tedious. By the time he had finishing, everyone was tired, and the King said:

"We will continue this afternoon as there still are outstanding witnesses." He was about to get up, but the judge got up first and asked for permission to speak.

He told everyone that he was aware that they had not put forth the best of themselves since the Tribunal had nothing to offer that the others could learn. So, moving forward, after examining the witnesses, each of the two presenters would defend their position again. This time with arguments that would carry more weight but take less time. While saying that, he looked at the Defender, who felt alluded to and wanted to speak, but the King took the matter for finished, and said:

"Fine. We will continue this afternoon."

As soon as the King left the hall, the rest of them surrounded the judge, speaking at the same time over one another. But, at that moment, the King returned, and they were all immediately cut off, and he said to the judge:

"Your intervention seems right to me. I want conclusions to be drawn, and you are supposed to be the best at it. So, get to thinking and working." And he turned to leave again. It seemed that the King was slow to think, but he was, nevertheless, thinking.

In the afternoon, they all returned. The Spirit of the Judge was watching everything and everyone, getting closer to one or another. He discovered that adverse comments were being directed against the one who played the Judge's role. The names they called him by were not nice. It seemed that they were afraid of him, for that is how people act in the presence of someone powerful.

In the afternoon session of the Tribunal, the following emerged. The presiding judge – the Judge – was seated in a superior seat of the hall, from where he could see everything, including all the people. He could also observe all the signs and winks that the others were sending to each other. It is given that in a trial, when someone who is speaking and has an assistant, they agree on the signs before starting so that the assistant can remind the speaker if they forget something. And that was what they were doing, but at a certain moment, the Judge stopped the Tribunal and said:

"In this Tribunal, no more signs will be shared. We all know this custom well, although it is only practiced in the Capital since, in rural areas, the Judge does not have an assistant. But this seems to be a reproduction of the kind of signs that are to please the public in a fiesta. However, as this is necessary for some people, I suggest the following."

"It would be better if the assistant sits next to the accuser or defender. And it does not matter whether there are one or two persons there. Or, if the assistant is sitting away, and has to be consulted, he is then called, they speak with him and hear what he has to say to them, and then the assistant retires. That way, everything will be clearer, since it is a known fact that pre-agreed signs can be forgotten and that sometimes the meaning can be taken for a different meaning." Everyone seemed satisfied with the suggestion.

They all thought that this new method was suitable, and so the witnesses were called and examined one after another. They did not say anything new, but each repeated what the Accuser and Defender had previously spoken. It was their turn to speak again, but just before they did, the Judge, again, took to saying:

"As the Judge, I must guide the Tribunal. One would think that we are deciding a case against the rural Judge. So put yourself in his shoes and stop being Judges of the Capital. What is being decided in this case is the agreed deal and not the sale itself. And, in this case, it was done in the way that people are not familiar with." He fell silent. The others seemed to be in agreement with him.

He passed the turn to the Accuser – or Prosecutor – who had now changed his arguments. Instead of passing the blame onto the untrained Judge, he laid it on the one who bought the land as he, knowing in advance what was planted there, had intended to partly compensate himself with the paid-in capital. He said nothing and intended to keep the profit of another man's work. The Judge said that he fell into the other man's trap because, he argued, when he bought the land, he already counted on that money as he was under the impression that the seller had increased the price for that reason.

When the Defender's turn came, he also changed his argument. He said that the seller had acted in bad faith since he had not mentioned anything as he was on the receiving end. Only after harvesting was finished and sold well, he raised the claim to ensure the legality of what was done. Surely, he would not have done the same if the harvest had been poor, and there would have been losses to be had.

He considered and put arguments forward that he had actually deceived the Capital Judge himself, that he, in some way, managed to get him not to dig deeper to learn the facts for himself by calling the buyer to learn his position. Then he introduced something new:

"Nor was it complied with what the Law provides, which is, in case of doubt, the opinion of the Principal of the Community will be obtained. So, with a false argument, he wanted to appropriate the legitimate owner's work. Because, although the crop had been planted when he sold the land when it was growing, it had to be tended to and helped by cleaning, watering, and clearing up animal muck. All so that he had food later." These arguments pleased everyone and, of course, made it difficult for the presiding Judge, for it left very little space for him to resolve this case justly. Regardless, he did not show any displeasure when his colleagues sang the same song.

When everyone had finished speaking, it was already late. The King, whilst rising, indicated that they would be called back soon on another day because he could not make it the next day. He said to the Judge:

"Think carefully about what your decision is going to be. And consult – how you say it? – the person who answers your Prayer. He understands that this work is important." And he left. Everyone expected him to return, but he did not.

The Spirit of the Judge observed the one who had the role of the Tribunal Judge, who was himself in the Dream. He also saw everyone leave, and saw he himself return to the body of the real judge –one of flesh and bones – who was reclined on the seat and sleepy. Of course, the time it all had taken was not long; it could have been an hour. That is to say that the Tribunal hearing had taken all day, but, in reality, it had only been like an hour of dreaming. He entered the body, came back to consciousness, and straightened himself. His body ached from lousy posture, and he was feeling exhausted, but he still made time to pray before going to bed. The HIGHEST, his Lord, said to him:

"Rest for the night. And write down everything that has been said and what you have seen so that you do not forget. And keep in mind that the trial is not over yet."

Three days had passed before the judge sensed that he was going to continue seeing and hearing the Tribunal again that night. And that it had still remained unfinished. And so it happened that same night, after having prepared what was necessary, he laid down waiting for the call. The call came and woke him up after three hours of sleep. He got up.

He wet his hands and face and sat down comfortably so as not to end up with the pain in his back as had happened on the previous occasion and waited. Soon, he entered a sleep-like state in which his Spirit shifted to the place where the Tribunals were held.

He saw everyone enter. The last one to enter, as befits, was the King. He watched everyone take their seats. Then the King declared the Tribunal open, and everyone's eyes were now staring at the Judge.

He, however, spoke the following:

" See, my Lord," he addressed the King. "The matter of the Tribunal is not at all clear yet, and, as the Judge, I have to clarify some things before passing sentence. Since I cannot visit the place where the events that were considered occurred and since everything is hearsay, I find myself limited to only having an opportunity of asking some questions in order to clarify the points that I consider obscure." He turned to the Accuser – or Prosecutor – and spoke to him. "You have chosen a person to hold responsible for everything, but have you done it for a good reason or just for sympathies? Because, at first, you indicted the Rural Judge, but later, you blamed the buyer. I wish to point something out as I need clarification. Doesn't the Accuser – or the Prosecutor – have to defend Justice itself, without taking sides? And, if he takes sides, does he not have to always side with the public interest? Why have you abandoned the first reason that was of public interest? Was it – basing on one particular individual – the lack of experience of the Rural judges?"

Everyone was startled and did not know where to turn from those questions. The Accuser called his two witnesses to consult with – this sort of thing was done for the first time – and they clarified what they were asked. The Accuser turned to the Judge and said:

"Mr. Judge, we understand your point of view, and we continue to say that it is preferable to proceed with the first argument, which is to hold responsible the rural judge. He had no training, and it is better to claim against the one who had wicked ideas of stealing the property of others."

The Judge then turned to the Defense and said:

"I also want clarification regarding this. You defend the cause of someone who claims to have been robbed, as well as of that who later has been served Justice. Which of the two causes is the one you defend? Because if it is the first one, it cannot be done as he already has a judgment passed. And if it is the second one, it cannot be done in a Tribunal but, instead, by calling for the Superior."

The Defender did what his learned colleague, the Accuser, did just moments before, that is to say, he called the two witnesses of his who, as you know, were also Judges. They discussed between the three of them what their response should be, and one of them answered:

"You see, Mr. Judge, we maintain that the two support the same cause because if no one had been harmed, no claim would have been presented. And, if no court Judgment had been issued, the actions of the other would have been unlawful. Therefore, we continue supporting both arguments."

After that, the Judge asked the King for permission to retire for a Prayer, and the King said:

"I asked you to do so before coming back here. Now it is wasting our time."

The Judge patiently responded:

" See, my Lord, I had to get the answers to my questions, which have now been given to me. There would have been one Sentence without those answers, and there may be a different sentence with having had them."

The Kind understood this as said:

"Go. But do not take long."

And the Judge left.

His Spirit, however, remained in the hall, so it saw the King call his Minister of Justice over and ask him:

"Do you think that he really communicates with someone so wise that can give him the right answers for all the Tribunals? For throughout his long life, there will have been many."

The minister answered:

"I do not know, my Lord. But I can tell you that the other day the Principal of the Temple himself approached him to congratulate him and asked him to visit him at the Temple because he needed to ask him for advice. From this, I understand that he who knows these matters well believed it." The King was left lost in thought.

When the Judge returned, his face showed great concern. They all noticed it and became concerned too. They had begun to experience curious things; it was noticeable – in their gestures and in the way they spoke – that they started to see the Judge as if he were a born leader. A Chief that no one had named but who was gradually impressing himself onto others. And, among those others was someone as superior as the King himself who had already been asking for things from him instead of ordering him.

Taking the floor, the Judge greeted everyone standing up and then sat down and began to speak. That was a little strange since the Judge always read his Judgment standing up. But it seemed that this process had become a ground for making changes, as well as everyone, thought that considering that he was an old man, he probably could not support himself for long, so no one protested it. As for the King, he did not know much difference, so he did not take notice of it either. The judge started to speak:

"You see, the whole Tribunal was concerned with what is governed by the barter laws. As you all know, there are two of those." Nobody knew them as they were all from the Capital, where the money circulated. Everyone was looking at each other, and so the judge, after keeping quiet for a moment to focus attention, continued. "The first one states that any two parties are free to make a deal without any type of pressure or coercion. The latter is essential because, if any of the parties were to endure any pressure fearing that otherwise, the deal will fall through, it would be an imposition. Therefore, that would constitute an act of force that we call robbery. But remember that the word 'barter' involves equality."

"The second one is that, once the exchange deal is closed without any particularities, none of the parties can go back on the things that have been exchanged. And if one wishes to go back on something, it will be a matter of reaching a new deal. You see, if there were conditions, this would not be a barter but, rather, an agreement between the parties. But, in that case, it would have nothing to do with what we are discussing here."

"This second kind of deals," he addressed the Judges, " happens a lot in the city. Here, things are left in exchange for others with the condition that they are durable, or that they function in a certain way, or if a price that is charged is for the subsequent sale and other similar dealings. All of these are agreements which, as Judges, you know well, give us a lot of headaches. They make these agreements by word and by trusting each other instead of in writing, and then that word that was agreed on changes." The judge continued talking. "Thus, the rural judge, with this basic knowledge, considered that once one receives the money and the other receives the property deed, the barter deal had been closed, and all was finalized. If someone later brings a claim regarding the kind of barter deal, they were not to be heard."

"Justice only intervenes into a barter deal when there has been a manifest of bad faith or malicious deceit with prejudice to the estimated value. For example, selling sick cattle and hiding the fact that it is sick. For this reason, barter deals in these cases are allowed the cool-off period of one moon to bring their claim and annul the deal. However, in these cases, there would always be a full revocation of the deal and not a partial one. In this case, this man, the claimant, not only left the given time period to expire, but he did not return the money to recover his land either. Instead, he had already spent it."

"With respect to the consideration regarding the rural judge's experience or knowledge, and that a rural judge is considered inferior to that of the capital, it must be taken into account that, when an appointment of a judge is made, the only procedure that is carried out is an interview with the Principal. The Principal determines if a candidate has the capacity or not through a few questions which explore his reasoning. If, of course, his thinking is in harmony with the Principal's own, the judge is appointed and given jurisdiction. That sort of process, of course, is insufficient."

"But we must also admit that, in the Justice system, things like influence also play a role. If you are the son of so and so or if you have money or a certain position, and you are interested in a particular post, you call on someone who can help you with the interview. And so you leave there with less money in the bag but with a job that will be bringing food to your table forever."

"All the Judges should spend some time with one of the old judges, learn how they think. The magnificent Judges who we know as Masters – as they are recognized as that – should have a duty under Justice to take on some as students to mentor, so that later they come out as wise as their Master. So that all the wisdom and experience accumulated over so many years are not lost."

"But there is something that I consider even more important. It is said that the Judges are the representatives of the King. This, I tell you, is not true. If it were so, the King would be misrepresented. You see, the Judges have nothing to do with the Power of the King. Their function is to administer justice, which is to say it is managing the coexistence among the people of the Community. They are presented with a great number of problems that have nothing to do with the King's Power, whether it would be military and that of the various ministers. The judges have to support these people in everything so that they are safe in the knowledge that they can request their help if it becomes necessary."

"You see, a case can be argued that, if someone who considers himself wronged goes to a Judge to ask him for Justice against some folly of someone who is in Power, and if that Judge has no one to turn to in order to acquire justice to the one who has been harmed, we will find that Justice does not exist."

"It is clear that the power and the powerful who have a

lot of money, in many cases, perpetrate serious harm against people who have little ways of protecting themselves. And, following that and not knowing who to turn to, they have to endure the damages for the rest of their lives. The abuses they are subjected to by soldiers when they come to collect the taxes or when they go out to do training and pass near communities are examples of this."

"It is pointless to protest against the military's command as it always finds reasons for what has been done. And if it does not have a reason, one is sought out or manufactured. And, like that, people are always the ones who are subjected to suffering. It would not be like that if the harmed person knew that the Judge could turn to the Power of the King and the various ministers so that justice is done."

"Being confident before proceeding that you will be listened to with respect and not badmouthed or mistreated for filing complaints and claims. Knowing that, if someone dares to treat you in a bad way, their position will be taken away, and your matter will be solved. Justice must be effective."

As the Judge was speaking, everyone was becoming nervous, even the King himself. He stopped him and said:

"Hang on, Judge. I think you are going too far. You are

not saying that my ministers might be unfair, are you?"

The judge, looking straight at him and then lowering his head as a sign of respect, said:

"Yes, my Lord. And you know some of the instances. And many others do not reach you because they do their job well."

The King did feel like giving out a command at this point but wanted to continue listening, so he said:

"Very well, we shall speak later. Now, continue."

"In the countryside, those who are wronged are very frightened and rarely file lawsuits against those of importance. And if they do, it is the Judges themselves, knowing the result, that try to avoid it and reject them. Here, in the Capital, they have more confidence, and as, being closer, they are more likely to be considered, and it happens with relative frequency. The one who is powerful and happens to make some mistake, they cover it up, using violence, so that no one learns about it." The judge raised a second issue. "You will see," he was addressing everyone, but, in particular, the King who was present there, "that the number of Judges is insufficient in the countryside, while in the Capital, there are plenty. Here there are numerous districts, and some of them even have the capacity for cover when one judge falls ill. But what happens in the rural world, where there is one judge for a large county?"

"They have the same right as those living in the Capital. They pay the same taxes, they live in the same territory, they are of the same race, and they have the same beliefs. And they have the same King. So why Justice is not the same? Why is there Justice in the Capital but not in provincial towns? That is why, as a Judge, I dispense Justice.

"You see, just as there is a Principal in each community, there should be a Judge for it too. Naturally, the Communities are small, and it would not take anything more than splitting a set a number of people among judges to serve. This would mean that when there are disputes – since there aren't many people – their conflicts could be resolved quickly."

"For this reason, it is estimated that a Judge could not have more than three to five Communities. You see, a Judge must know all the parts of his jurisdiction well as he is the authority..." The Judge continued. "For this reason, I consider that a Judge does not represent the King at any time. Furthermore, I state that, since it is not only about judging but also about providing clear ideas, I will say that..."

"First, the Justice system must have a different organization from the current one. It should have a maximum of three ranks, these being the Rural Judge, the Capital Judge, and the Government Judge, or, instead, the Judge of the King serving for the Government."

When he said this, all the heads were up as they showed interest in the subject. So he continued explaining.

"The Rural Judge will have the jurisdiction over a specific region and the Communities it houses, and he will be the only one who will have the right to intervene in this area. He will be an experienced man of impeccable honesty; if he is ever lacking, he will step down himself as an unequivocal condition of his appointment."

"To regulate and ensure this — as well as to ensure that no one is left without Justice — there will be a chief overseeing the work of all the local Judges. He will visit each Community once a year. If anyone makes a complaint about the Rural Judge, this chief will study the case, and his Judgment will then be irrevocable. He, as a chief, will have the power to annul the Sentences passed by the Rural Judges."

"It also needs to be ensured that this Chief of the rural Judges is appointed on merits and wisdom. He will also be familiar with the lands which he will be overseeing. He will be selected and appointed from among all the rural Judges. It will not be done in a way where a new Judge from the Capital comes to be given that position or because he is the son of so and so. Or because someone in power wants it. That would be an injustice. The rural world must have its Justice system managed independently of the Capital."

"Knowledge of the problems that the rural world faces and how the people who live there think will be required. As well as familiarity with the particular customs that exist in each area and which may cause people to react to the same thing differently."

"There is an even more important matter, regardless if one is of Ethiopian origin or not. As it turns out, in the rural world, at the moment, many people are of Egyptian origin. Little by little, they are imposing their customs and ways of living on us because nobody is there to ensure Justice."

"Whilst it is true that our men and women seem a little behind in some respects when contrasted with the world of the Egyptians, that does not matter for they are ours, and we must protect them. Since it turns out that they, the Egyptians, know languages and some scriptures whilst ours do not, they have many laws whilst ours only have their understanding and customs. And so without having our Law and a Judge who can protect them using the rule of Law, many a time they are subjected to their will."

That new issue that the judge had started to discuss caught everyone's attention, especially the King's, who interrupted him and said:

"Stop for a moment and clarify in more detail what it is that you are talking about."

"My Lord, in your Kingdom, there are more inhabitants of Egyptian origin than of our own. This, in itself, is dangerous because, if someday someone from the other side comes with interests in our lands, they will find help among their own."

"They are peaceful, and they do not cause any problems so that they are left in peace in lands that now belong to the Ethiopians but that in the past were theirs. They pay their taxes and respect the laws when the Authorities are present."

"But when it is not present, they impose their customs, they continue to worship their Gods, they continue to celebrate their religious festivals with blood sacrifices, and they continue to abide by their own laws as they are the majority. We do not have an institution that would impose our customs on them. Yes, we have the soldiers. Yes, they inhabited territories that, in the past, were theirs. But, where they are, they command."

"It is not about turning them into enemies but, rather, that our own are protected against the abuses of the Egyptian Laws that they impose and apply to our people as if on Foreigners on the Ethiopian land. This matter has been reported previously, but it was of no use. When the

Authority presents itself, the order is restored. But when it leaves and does not return for several moons again, those who live there have to just bear not having a local Judge." The judge deemed the clarification for completed and continued with the subject matter. "See, the Chief of the Rural Judges will be overseeing of the appointments as well as ensuring that everyone has the required relevant experience. When he needs to appoint a new judge, he will place him in one Community for some time. Then another one to spend some time there too. And then the third one. So that by the time he has finished his placements, he will have already gotten to know three Communities and will possess the minimum knowledge needed to carry out his mission."

"There will be separate judges in the Capitals. This is because the problems that arise from the increases of the number of people in the Capital do not happen in the countryside. Therefore, the people who live in the Capital will have to be more open-minded and more educated so that everyone knows the trade and the different forms of measurement that get used. As well as languages so that Justice does not have to depend on an intermediary in order to be able to listen as well as to make itself heard. Because the one who stands in the middle often converts into a judge."

"You all know the case when one told another through an intermediary to tell him where a treasure was or, if no, he would kill him. The other told him, and the intermediary said to the person who asked that he would not tell them and that he would rather be killed. And so they did. And when everyone had left, the intermediary went and found the treasure and kept it for he deemed it to be the prize of his work."

"In order for justice to be achieved, the Judge must have enough culture in him and be independent of all the others. We know that intermediaries are easy to bribe and, thus, the one with the least scruples will be the one who agrees to be bought. Then he who trusts the Justice system will learn that the interpreter speaks against him." Some nodded their heads as he said that. The judge continued. "The Judges of the Capital will be divided into districts, and it will be ensured that each one can only intervene and serve justice in their own district. That way, if in any particular district, many are discontent with the Justice system, it will be apparent that the Judge is not good at serving it."

"It must also be kept in mind that Justice in the Capital starts not with the rural concepts of barter or exchange, but with Commerce based on buying, selling and doing business, but, above all, on coexistence. Many lawsuits are arising from the limited housing issue and from residents having interfered with each other and other such things that do not occur in rural areas."

"The Judges of the Capital will also have a chief, a Chief Judge. His preparation and experience must be higher than that required of a regular Judge of the Capital. His mission will be to visit and be present in each of the districts, getting to know the entire city, all the Principals, and all the merchants and other influential people closely. In this way, he will be able to learn when someone with their power or their money tries to do business with the Justice system."

"This Chief Judge of the Capital will not have their own district but, rather, he will be overseeing the entire Capital. He will have three Judges in his charge as assistants whose identity will not be revealed. When they come to sit in and watch the courts as if they were regular members of the public – sometimes they will even be witnesses or take part in some trials – they will report everything to their boss. We all know that, if someone has something to hide from their boss, they will be sure not to reveal it in their presence."

"But this is not only because it has to be controlled but because it has to be continuously learning. So the Rural Judges, as well as the Judges of the Capital, from time to time, will receive instruction on new matters that have come to light. As well as on new laws that have been passed or new ways of doing things that were being done differently before. Things that need to be corrected. These are the things that the two Chiefs – that of Rural Judges and that of Judges of the Capital – will oversee and carry the responsibility to ensure that Justice that is being served is the best that it can be."

"Of course, all these trials are to be carried out, in both the rural territories and in the Capital, in civil courts. It will be acknowledged that crimes of blood answer to the Authority. For these crimes, wherever they are committed, there will have to be specially prepared Judges who will also have the specific authorizations to execute or to confiscate property, or to banish from the territory, or whatever else that the Authority has reserved for them."

"These Judges will be based in the Capital, but they will have to travel to where may be necessary instead of making everyone, guilty and innocent, come to a place that is not their own. And, in the end, they lose their lives because they do not know the customs or the language or the way of speaking. If a Blood Trial is to be held in rural areas, this Judge will take as his assistant the Judge of that Community, unless, of course, the Judge himself is the subject of the matter. In that case, he will take the Chief of the Rural Judges for an assistant, for no one can know the background or the people better than him."

"But it will need to be ensured that these special Judges depend on the Authority and not on the Minister of Justice. They will be independent, and the Authority will be their right hand which they will have their fists closed on and, when they put an order a place, it will be executed."

"There is yet another layer. The one where the Authority itself must submit to the scrutiny of courts. It is a given that there are many cases of abuse of power, not only in the military sense but also in the form of an excessive time that is taken to serve justice. This results from the complications that they put in place so as not to safeguard Justice as it should be done. As well as from the place where the King imparts Justice." He looked directly at the King and told him, "I understand that here the truth has to be told, and this truth is known to all. For this reason, there will be a rank of Judges that will be made up only of Principals, each of whom will be responsible for each sector of the kingdom. It will be made up of twelve parts."

"The King – his person and his family – will have a Minister as a representative in cases of absence or unavailability; the military chief, as an authority – but solely military – who will oversee security. There will also be five Ministers who will be in charge of the civil matters and five Ministers in charge of the Spiritual matters. They will all be appointed directly by the King. But their duty will be to look after not only the interests of the King but be responsible for the people's interests too."

"It will be made up of the three parts. One will be that of the military, another of the civilian, and one more, that of the Spiritual," the judge repeated it for all to understand. "You will see that I have included the Spiritual. That is because, in the Temple, there is now a charge, which is a commercial element, as well as it has influence and has dealings with it too. Therefore, someone who answers directly to the King must control this kind of power."

"I have also spoken about the military previously. I want to make it very clear that the military will only be responsible for the defense of the territory and for maintaining order within it as well as for blood crimes. But it will certainly no longer be responsible for the tax collection."

"It needs to be kept in mind that this is the essential element of the Kingdom. If it does not work well, the rest will not work either for the people who depend on the King – as well as his Ministers – will not be paid. The collection of taxes will depend directly on one of the civil ministers. Its own institution will have to be established, independently of the military whose function now is very clearly elsewhere."

"See, right now, there is a large number of different terms that apply to the collection of taxes. There are many justifications for these too. This causes many people in the Capital and rural areas to be unfamiliar with the subject and, consequently, they always end up paying too much. For not knowing when, how much, or how they must pay, and, on top of it all, who to pay to."

"It is known – and currently there is no remedy for that – that in both the rural areas and in the Capital as well as in some sectors of it, they go on to collect taxes from several different places in the Kingdom. They do it without prior notice, and they demand quantities that nobody has. They keep all they can of it, and nobody dares to protest. Since there is no Justice system in place that could stop this abuse of Power – nor is there anyone sensible enough to put order – almost all the tax that has to be delivered to the King is lost at the hands of those who collect but do not deliver."

"It may seem that, as a result, there are three classes of Judges. Still, in practicality, there is only one, since each chief – that of the rural jurisdiction, the jurisdiction of the Capital, and the chief of tax collection management – will answer to the Minister of the civil matters."

"The second minister, that of the Military, and the

third minister, that of the Spiritual, will be wholly governed by the King or the King's minister who, in his name, will oversee the administration of Justice. It will be done in such a way that he will only act through the three ministers. He will not only serve justice but will, in effect, control the entire territory or the Kingdom," the judge continued. "The only one that does not seem to have much importance is the one who actually has the most, the Minister of the Spiritual. You see, people without strong Spirituality will soon be overtaken and dominated by their enemies since they have no place where to upkeep their personal values and virtues. In our case, this is of the highest importance, for we have a large number of people from Egypt who continue to worship their Gods and their idols and, therefore, continue to answer to the power of the Priests of Egypt."

"It is known that every year Egyptian Priests come to visit their people and give them the Religious support they need. You can see that, even after having lost a war, the Egyptian people continue to be united in their Religion."

"And our own, my Lord," he addressed the King, "increasingly lack spiritual foundations. Before, the spiritual teaching was compulsory, and it was free. Now only those who can afford to pay can visit the Temple. And I assure you that there are very few and, of course, these are those that are not destined to suffer the struggle under the imposition of the Egyptian religions in rural areas." The judge continued. "Provide strong support to the Spiritual, and you will see how our young will spread their own practices throughout the territory. For right now, in rural areas, they are enticed by the color and sound of music and the food and drink of the feasts of the Egyptian Gods. And they believe in them."

The King and all the others were surprised by this and said:

"Hang on. It certainly has me interested a lot because it seems logical. But tell me, how will all this be paid?"

The Judge responded to the King by saying:

"You see, my King, the funding is what gives force to the Power. It will be done as follows: from now on, in rural areas, a fixed sum will have to be paid – as a tax – to the King for each Tribunal. That way, people will not bring claims to Court without it being really important."

"As coexistence is vital, having to pay a court tax will make them think about it twice, and they may settle among themselves instead of paying. But the expenses have to be specified and must be a fixed figure. It will serve to pay for the duration that it will last, the relocation of the Judge, and for all the tests that have to be carried out. But, in any case, a maximum of two percent of the value of the litigated will be charged, one of which will be the tax and the other to cover expenses."

"As for the Capital, as more specialization and higher preparation are required, it will be three percent; taxes of which will be two percent while the expenses will be the same as in the countryside, the one percent."

"As for the Chief Judges, they will not charge anything because they answer to the King, and they will only attend to the matters among the King's people. The same will apply to the Chiefs of both Rural and Capital Judges. They will be awarded a fixed salary from the King, which will be set by the minister that appoints them."

"The reason for this is to see to it that no one loses out and that the trivial things that are brought to Tribunals diminish, leaving more time to serve justice on the important matters. These will also be charged for." When everyone thought that the case had been finalized, the Judge spoke again. "You see, my Lord, no one should benefit from Justice for Justice must be free. It is something that comes from the people themselves and is granted to the King for redistribution among humankind."

"Every year, the rural regions, as well as the Capital which the King has the disposal of, will have returned the amounts collected from them in forms of taxes and expenses. This way, one day, the poor who can hardly afford to eat and others who do not have the means to seek Justice for it is too expensive, will have Justice served to them for free. The way that it will be done is that they pay first and then have it returned to them."

The King understood what was being said to him, and said:

"It does not seem right to me. The one who does not have anything is to be served Justice for free and no charge to be taken for it. Neither the rural Judges nor those of the Capital or those of the Principals will charge anyone like that who prove their lack." They all agreed. There was a smile on the Judge's face, and the King, having seen it, understood that he was forced to intervene. He said to him, "It worked out well for you. We will be deciding on something again soon. This time it will be THE RULERS."

Once the Tribunal had finished, everyone got up to go. The King ordered that everything is written down and that they would all reconvene again in a few days to sign the conformity as witnesses that it is a Just Judgment ordered by a Just Judge. He looked at him again and left.

The Judge's Spiritual energetic body returned to his physical body, and when he regained consciousness, he said a Prayer to the HIGHEST, to his Lord, who said:

"My Faithful Servant, put everything that has gone through your mind in writing. For it has been a dream, and so that humanity can learn about it. Now rest. I will be calling you again another day, and you will dream again."

The Third Dream

On one occasion, while the judge was still serving as a Judge in the Capital, the Chief Judge decided to hold an event similar to the one he had experienced years ago when he held a Tribunal for the Gods. He decided to have it in the place where conflicts were commonplace, and the pay was less, the Souk. Only this time, he wanted to hold it in the Capital itself because that way, he did not have to move away from his workplace, as well as it saved the other Judges who he wanted to include from having to do the same.

When he started putting the idea into action, he began talking it over with other Judges. In the end – as they could not reach an agreement – of his own discretion, he used the power of his office to establish which ones of the Judges he wanted to train in what he came to call a Masters of Judges training. It was only a manner of calling it since he included himself in the list to serve in the same position which he had been given by The Judge on the previous occasion.

The judge, who had heard of the matter but had not been consulted, was ordered to present himself to the Chief Judge, with whom he did not get along. This man who represented Justice was continually committing an injustice towards the judge; he was made to pay ten percent of what he charged in all his Tribunals just for being allowed the privilege to practice in the Capital since he was a rural judge.

So the judge was called. The call did not seem fair, for he had learned that others had been consulted and that, after consulting some of them, he had invited some but not the others. Whilst he had not been consulted at all. However, out of obedience to authority, he went. He found it difficult for a task having to listen to the Chief Judge of all the Judges appoint him as a Judge of the case.

The judge wanted to protest since he was the least of the Capital's Judges. Not because of his age or experience, of which he had considerably more than many of those who were there. More because he had only arrived here at the Capital a short while ago, and the position he was appointed to correspond to any other but him.

However, given the experience that he had demonstrated in the previous tribunal, the Chief Judge decided that the invited judge would fill this role. To the great disappointment of those – and there were many – who were willing to occupy the position of a Judge in this tribunal that was being brought. And so it was.

The judge had to set out the arrangements of who would be the assistants to argue the Defense, who would be the ones who would argue the charge, and who would be the witnesses. He thought he would also have to appoint the head Accuser, but he learned that the Chief Judge had this position reserved for himself.

Once the judge realized that all of the assistants were Judges – for some of them, he did not know – he concluded that the Chief Judge should not serve in that position. Otherwise, he would end up with a situation where everyone's expressed opinions would be subject to what the Chief Judge wanted or did not want, for everyone else was subordinate to him.

Having shared out the appointments, he confronted the Chief Judge and told him that, if he wanted him to serve as a Judge, in this case, he could not serve a role of a head Accuser. He explained that, since he was a Superior to everyone there, both himself and others out of respect to his opinions would have difficulty arguing their positions for they were his subordinates. The Chief Judge, feeling flattered, agreed and gave up the position, but said to him:

"Fine. But assign me a different position in which I can serve. Just observing, without participating, does not suit me."

The Judge responded:

"You see, you will preside over the Tribunal as though you were the King himself. When appropriate, you will alter or cut in or ask for a more thorough explanation. And, of course, insist that others improve at their work. Because, above all and everyone, the Authority must always be present."

The Chief Judge liked it and said:

"This suits me. I accept."

This is how the judge achieved to enable himself to pick the people he wanted. He chose two Judges as accusers and ordered them to bring three witnesses from home. He did the same with the other two Judges that he appointed as defenders, but gave them the condition that the witnesses were to be of different social classes, not members of the same family, and not linked to the Judges in any way.

This somewhat inconvenienced the other Judges who already had everything organized, but they liked the principle and thought that the handling of the matter began well. They were determined to invite the King to sit in this matter but, when the judge learned of their intention, he said no. The tribunal that was about to be heard would be deciding on the matter of the Royals, and the King may not be best pleased, which could cause everyone to end up with their heads on the ground.

The Chief Judge, who had not chosen the subject matter of the Tribunal himself but, instead, gave the judge the task of selecting it, was now a little worried. He thought it would be better to leave this subject for another occasion for fear that the King may not like the idea. He approached the judge to ask him what it was that they were occupying the time that they had to dedicate to serving Justice with. Still, he did not dare to turn back on the decision since everything was now organized as well as it would leave him in a disadvantageous position and may cause him to lose authority.

At first, it was also thought that there would be someone there to represent the King's position so that he could have something said on his behalf, but then it was determined that it would not be convenient as well as it could be displeasing for the royalty, and they did not want to seek out problems. So The King would have to be prosecuted in his absence.

It was decided to look for a specific figure to symbolize the King so that things could be considered and determined with some level of precision. They chose a King known by all due to the shared history they all had. This King was noted for his cruelty and his continuous wars in pursuit of conquering land and property.

The trial had initially been thought to last three days but reserving the possibility that it would have to be extended open. To ensure that things are done well, it was decided not to have a time limit and, if the circumstances demanded, it would be temporarily suspended, resuming it on another occasion. So it was to everyone's surprise when the Judgement was arrived at within two days.

The trial began in a country house that the Chief of the Judges had near the capital. As such, when all the Judges arrived and installed themselves there, the trial began.

At first, there was a lot of noise but little use because each one wanted to show off in front of the Chief Judge, and he himself wanted to show off in front of his subordinates, so the matter had not progressed. All but the presiding Judge were doing it. Only when the whole of the morning was wasted that someone realized that the judge was not partaking. So, when he suddenly spoke with a loud voice, everyone looked at him. He was watching them all, studying them, and when they asked him about why he was not participating, he replied:

"When the tribunal begins, I will have it ready what I have to say. At the moment, it is, apparently, your turn to say what you have to say." Having heard this, they all realized that they were speaking without listening or being listened to, and, little by little, they started taking their seats and positions and adopting demeanors appropriate to Judges.

The judge – as Judge of the case – stated who was being judged. He kept in mind that he should be careful so that no kind of resentment was expressed or anything that could be interpreted as an insult towards those who were the rulers at the time was said.

For this reason, he had chosen an ancient figure that everyone knew. Not personally, but remembered. One that did not belong to the family or lineage of the current King but, instead, to another family, no one of which had remained.

The introduction was short. The idea was formulated that the king that was being prosecuted was absent. He had been in power for twenty years, and he had fought six wars with his neighbors. He had rid of vast areas of land of their inhabitants, both vegetation and animals, and turned them into deserts.

The trial began differently now that the judge took command. After his brief presentation, others began to speak. They did this in order as well as in adherence to the rules that were in place. But something unusual happened that made this trial, like the one before, different, and served as a lesson for everyone to take away.

On the first break, the judge felt the need to pray and, as he did so, the HIGHEST answered him and told him to do three things:

"First, talk to the Principal to split the matter into three different concepts: who has the right to appoint a king, who has to be a king, and what powers does a king have."

"Second, you have to direct the accusers, including the Principal. They ought to approach it in a way that is not a criticism of actions but, instead, address the concepts. The concepts of what they have done and what is still left to be done."

"And, as for those who are defending, they ought to contribute valuable points and to not limit themselves to only dismissing what the others will have said. You, as the Judge of the case, must disallow – on both sides – what is not important so that, in the end, there is only left what is worth the bother."

And that is how the Judge approached it. He soon realized that the murmur of approval began to spread. But they did not take kindly to someone that is not usually superior to them was telling them what they had to do. So the two defenders decided that they wished to impose their own criteria and present a series of evidence. When they said so, the judge agreed, and they had gone to consult with each other in private.

The way it was done was that the one who acted as the Judge only participated at the beginning. Not in the way that was customary then. This was to act as an investigator to see who was telling the truth. But, instead, as a listener.

The arguments were well presented and reasoned, but when the time came for the Judge to say no, they did not mind it that much. And so the work was coming to an e end.

The negative answer that the Judge gave made no sense, at least in appearance. But as will later be seen, a distinct approach was missing. An approach that would be different from how things were done at the time. After everyone had finished, including the Chief of the Judges, the Judge of the case asked for permission to retire. As everyone knew where he was going, no one objected and stayed awaiting his Judgment.

When the judge came back out of the room where he had been praying, according to what those who were waiting for him said later, he looked like someone else and gave out the impression of being somewhat absent. They asked him if he was all right. At times, the experience of the contact that the Judge was having with the HIGHEST was so pure that his human nature could hardly take it.

After a few minutes, the judge began to speak. Everyone was listening and were amazed at the wisdom that was being spoken through his lips.

The reasoning for who could name the King had been provided and that was another king in his absence. It would be the same king who would proclaim himself as such after having carried out an act of force. His explanation was as follows.

In the nation where the HIGHEST dwells – which is the nation in which he manifested as prophets throughout the lands – the only one who could name the King was HIGHEST himself. Because if the King were just and listened and obeyed him, it meant that the will of the HIGHEST in those lands would always prevail.

If, on the other hand, someone granted themselves the right to become a King but was not named as one by the HIGHEST, they would be reprimanded for the audacity. This would be done through the prophets who, instead of aiding them, would see to that their failures are reproached and that they are reprimanded publicly, for they have dared to disobey that who is all-powerful.

The King's obligations – on which more or less everyone agreed – were to protect the people, sustain and defend the nation, and work to give its people a better life.

The judge then proceeded to say the following:

"He who holds the position of a King is an administrator and, therefore, should not consider that everything belongs to him. Or that something can be given or taken away in his name. Or that Justice should serve his whim or be done when it is convenient to him. He who holds the position must consider that all are equal before the LORD. Therefore, when more is given to one than to the other, injustice is committed. While it may be true that some have more for intelligence and are naturally more gifted, it does not mean that they deserve more. It is a fact that everyone comes to this world and leaves it in the same manner. Therefore, the Administrator should ensure that everyone has rights and access to food, clothes, and place of shelter at the very least. And when all these basics are covered, everyone will be given the right and access to enjoy culture as well as an open path to the Temple where they can find and speak and listen to who they are really ought to serve."

"In addition," the judge continued, and everyone was listening to him. It was the third time that he had started to speak. "Among the obligations that the Kings have – if they have any at all – is to ensure that the one whom everybody must serve is known and talked about everywhere. And that the faith we follow is spread to all the parts of the kingdom. And so, following our customs, the young priests – in pairs – would have to be taught to walk our roads and speak to the people."

"In this way," the judge continued after pausing to give everyone a moment to understand his words. Upon hearing someone taking a deep breath, thus, indicating that they were about to interfere, he ended with saying, "Of course, all that was said applies when the King is a real King and not a person who had been given the position through the influences of the power groups or the military or the priests themselves. It applies where the person who was given the position was given it for possessing the proper merits."

"You see, an administrator ought to be unique in terms of his preparation for the position as well as in terms of his fidelity. The first thing he is ought to serve is his lord and not his own life or estate. That is how it should be with kings."

The judge fell silent, and no one else said anything, either. The Chief Judge approached him and said:

"To be truthful, I know that you have someone very special who dictates you the sentences, but I wish to say that this one, by far, is the best that I have known to come through your lips. However, I do not want anyone to repeat anything of what has been said here. And if someone repeats it, it will be denied by the others. And if anyone confirms it, you will go to jail with everyone else. I, myself, am the King's administrator and, therefore, fulfilling my duty to what has been said here, I put an end to this tribunal."

The Fourth Dream

After some time has passed, one day, the judge felt restless again. Being familiar with the symptoms, the judge knew that He wanted to communicate something to him. He also knew that this would occur at night for that how it always had been previously. That night, he prepared himself, remained calm, and prayed. When the time came, he got up, washed himself, and settled down, waiting for the dream-like state to come.

He saw his Spirit leaving his physical body and – very hurriedly – flying towards the King's palace. He saw himself entering and making his way up to another room – a room that he had never physically been to before. Once he descended, he started inspecting the detail of his surroundings. He walked up to the hall where the tribunal would be held and entered. There was nobody there yet, so he slowly walked across the room and saw that it had six large pillars that were set out in such a way that they formed a geometric figure, a hexagon. It is known that, in ancient times, this building style was typical. But, nowadays, they were usually built in the shape of either a square, or rectangle, or circle, but not in any other shape.

He soon saw how everyone, one after another, began to enter. They were talking among themselves. He then saw himself as one of the last ones to come in. Since he was not the main judge this time, he was not allowed to enter the palace until he was given permission to do so, for the guards had not been notified of his attendance. But, even so, he arrived before the King who, as is known, must be the last to enter and the first to leave.

They entered and sat down. The King opened the session by addressing the Minister of Justice, and saying:

"I want you to change some of the charges around but keep the same Judge for he seems to be the one who contributes the most. However, as no one is irreplaceable, if we see that the arrangement does not serve us, you appoint them to another position, and this first position is to be given to another. With this," he continued, "I am saying that no one is more important than anyone else and that being a defender, a witness, an accuser, or a judge is all the same. This is to preserve the representation of people's reality of life."

Everyone understood, and the judge began to speak. But the Minister of Justice wanted to show off, took the word from him and, for everyone's attention, read out about the previous tribunal and allegations and what had been decided at the end of it. Everyone showed acknowledgment and, when the King was about to answer, the judge said:

"My Lord, I think something has been forgotten."

Everyone found themselves trembling while the judge continued. "The last thing that was said previously and that is of great importance was not mentioned. That is that Justice would be free for all of those who do not possess any assets. Everyone attested this. As well as that they would not have to pay taxes or costs or the Judges' fee." The King affirmed it, and the Minister apologized while giving the judge a dissatisfied look. It was thought that this matter would not be returned to anymore, so no one went into the trouble of signing it. And, since it was not the time for signatures, it was arranged that everything that was said should be added as an addendum. Then the new Tribunal started the subject matter of which was poverty.

The Judge began by explaining that, in all countries, there were people who, for various reasons, were living in poverty. And that it was not acceptable that in some households it was lived in luxury, while in others there was not enough to eat. He also said that the King, while being the Ultimate person of the whole Kingdom and who had to watch over all that is under his reign, never carried direct responsibility for this matter. And that it could not be left in the hands of the rich and powerful for they never settled the issue and never did anything to remove this disparity even though they had the capacity. This provided a reason to think that there must have been some who had a vested interest in the existence of poverty.

The introduction was not well received because it involved them all. But, as they were already familiar with his approach from previous occasions, they let it be, and the accusers began their turn.

The accusers changed the direction which the Judge had set. They began to say that those who succumb to the vice of not working, who poorly administer their lives, who do not pay their debts, who cannot hold down a steady job, who were now working for a wage, and all the rest of them – he named many more vices – they were like that because life had this kind of path marked for them. And that they just had to come to terms with the luck that they have been awarded. He also said that, even though sometimes these people were given work and spoken to, whenever they were left to their devices, they did nothing to get themselves out of the misery.

One could easily notice that everywhere some lived well and that this was owing to their intelligence. And that when they put their intelligence to the service of others was when they prospered. They did that with commerce and construction and with manufacturing. They were the men who did not produce anything themselves, but they gave work to others. Hence, according to him, these men – who were few – were chosen ones, and had the right to live well when compared against the thugs who are used to being poor, who brought illnesses, and devoted themselves to feeding and living off robbery and mugging. And so, instead of offering alternatives, he began to defend the system to which everyone was nodding. Everyone but the Judge at whom the King was glancing from time to time.

The turn of prosecution's witness to put forward their case came, and the same line of presentation followed. He told of a made-up instance – which he later said to have lived – and that was no different to what the other had said:

"A well-off man who had put in the effort to study, who knew languages, mathematics, and astronomy, as well as had been a member of the Temple and had an inner voice, had prospered in such a way that he in no time became a Judge. However, he soon left the post, for he understood that it was more valuable to generate wealth for everyone, and he became a merchant. And a farmer and then a cattle dealer. Therefore, he had many men at his command, and it was great. Not only he had money and distributed it among the poor, but he also followed all the rules of generosity, and he seemed like an excellent example to everyone.

When the defenders' turn came to argue the issue, it seemed that they had no arguments to offer for they were all explicitly affirming with their heads what their learned friend had said, and who not only justified them all but also did it well.

They blamed the lack of culture, the Temple, the merchants, the taxes, the bad weather that spoiled crops, the low wages. They said that everything was costly. They also spoke about these people not having homes, not having access to clean water or clothes or medicines, while those around them had it all.

They discussed systems – they said they knew them well, but, in reality, they did not – that maintained poverty. It was due to bad luck or maybe because the gods wanted it that way. They also said that they used those that govern as a scapegoat and put the blame on them for everything bad happening to them. In the end, he stated that other governments sustained them because they served them as spies.

Once everyone finished, as they always did, they went out to eat. The Spirit of the Judge waited around for some time. Eventually, he had grown tired of it and went out for a walk around the courtyard. While walking, he saw the King eating accompanied by the Minister and two of the judges. That caught his interest, so he approached them and heard them speak of the Judge. The Minister was saying that he was a simple man who was not interested in serving in courts at all and that his only friends were justice and his people. He had no other friends among the judges, and, apparently, he always had a terrible time when he was in the Capital, and it seemed that this was the reason why he wanted nothing to do with it.

The King, however, addressed the other two:

"And what do you two think? Because it seems to me, in the matter of intelligence, he is invaluable."

And the others – one by one – tried to say that it may be so but not as much. They were also saying that he dressed inappropriately and that when he would come to town from his village, he would do it with an animal considered to be a farm animal and, therefore, not appropriate for a judge. And that those things are noticed, and that the profession is judged by it. But the King could be heard saying:

"Well, even so, I consider him very intelligent."

Seeing the royal approval, they all agreed but, inside, they all felt envious that someone had stood out to the King like that.

See, among those who feel that they are close to power, this is common. If someone stands out for something, they, instead of being happy for them, begin to consider them as a potential enemy. The danger only really exists in their minds, but it makes them nervous, and they start preparing attacks against him who, not long ago, did not even exist to them. Even though, in reality, all that is now had always been. But this is the nature of man; of a man who comes near the power."

When everything had been arranged for the afternoon session, and the end of the Tribunal was anticipated for everything seemed clear, just as the hearing was about to resume, the judge asked the King for permission to speak. He said:

"We seem to have endeavored to justify the way the things are now, but, in this way, we achieve nothing new and continue living in the same kind of misery. It would be good to think of means that would help us change things from what they are now so all can have a better life. Those who live in poverty and those who are surrounded by it. Or, at least, this is how I have I understood the King's wish." He turned to the Kind and said, "Please correct me if I am mistaken. But what I take from this Tribunal, as it stands, that nothing new that would help others was achieved."

The King pondered for a little while and said:

"As always, it seems that you are right. So I will wait a little while and, when I come back, I want solutions," he said. "I see, judge, that you have already said you Prayer because I understand that, from yourself, you do not have the intelligence nor the courage to speak like this."

The Judge responded:

"Indeed."

Everyone was giving the Judge evil looks, but none dared to say anything after the praise that the King himself had given him. They began to think and decided that, since it was getting late, that one speaker to represent each side would be enough. Two groups were formed – that for the accusation and for the defense – and, without trying to listen to each other's debate, they began to put the effort in their own work for they wanted to show off and be admitted right.

When the King entered and saw it, he smiled, for he saw that it was working. He said:

"If you need more time, tell me, and I shall come back later."

But, as he was told that they were ready, they all sat down to resume the hearing. Just as the accuser was about to start, the judge said:

"For the privilege that the King has given me to preside over this tribunal, I would like to see if, in his opinion, – and it is in his best interest – the King himself wishes to give us his opinion on poverty. Maybe he could tell us what he thinks about this matter because, up to now, we do not know. But it is necessary that those around him know what the King thinks if they want to be of help to him."

The King was pleased with the flattery and embarked

on the subject without once stopping to think that he may not come out victorious. He had a good opinion of himself, so he began by saying:

"As the King, I would like all men and women of this nation to have access to food, clothes, and a good life. As for the rest, as I appreciate that a difference in terms of the personal effort of each person should be acknowledged, this would come in once all of their necessities had been taken care of," and he fell silent.

Everyone was nodding so visibly that some of their heads nearly fell from the number of times they moved it. The Judge then said:

"We thank you. And now we can resume the Tribunal."

Some had to touch up their presentations. They thanked the judge for so cleverly revealing what the King thought.

When the Judge's turn came, his ideas were very confused, so he asked for permission to retire for Prayer. When the King told him no and that the Tribunal should continue, the judge said:

"Perhaps you think that everything comes out of my head, but it is not like that. I am just a rural judge, and I do not have the knowledge of many things. I know some things from being old, but not because I studied the Laws of Ethiopia. When I was young, I studied those of Egypt, but now that is of no use, knowing their origin, for they turned out to be the enemies."

The King looked at him and said:

"Are you trying to tell me that everything you tell us so accurately is because you are told these things when you pray? If so, then you should not be a Judge but, instead, serve in the Temple where you could help others much more in their Spiritual life."

The Judge respectfully – with his head bowed – replied:

"You see, everything I say that seems extraordinary is what I am told in the Prayer. As for your last point, I will tell you that I, myself, asked about that, and I was told:

'Your job is to serve Justice and not the Spiritual world. There, you have others who do the best with what they are allowed to, for the interference of power with the Temple matters has made it different from what it used to be.'

The King did not like that much, and so he said:

"Fine. We will see to it that the power of Religion and the Temple is the subject matter of the next tribunal. But, for now, as I know that we are not going to get anything out of you unless you say a Prayer, go, we will wait. However, do not forget that a King is waiting, so it is best that what you have to say after is important."

The judge understood the warning, so he went out to where he could – to an adjoining room – and began to pray.

Soon, the King entered and, seeing him on his knees and with his head on the ground, he left without saying a word. But he liked that someone had these convictions because, although he was a Young King, it was not his youth for which he stepped out of the customs of the elders.

When the judge came out, his face did not express much other than concern, and he said the following when his turn to speak came:

"I apologize to the King and the judges for having made you all wait, but you all know that I am only a rural Judge and that I never pass sentence without having said a Prayer and listened to the message from the one I deem as my Lord. Until now, he has always given me a Fair Sentence to pass. I am – in his hands – an instrument through which he delivers good to others. On this occasion, he has told me the things that I wish to repeat to you all. And I beg you that, if some things will not seem right to you, that you take issue with me but not with my Lord."

"He has told me to remind you that not even a King has the right to watch or listen to the prayer of others. He also said to me that there would not be much use of all the work that is being done here if the one who presides over it does not have the benefit of the others in mind as an end goal but only their own interest. When a threat is said, it seems that it is done by someone who can threaten but not by someone who can be a winner." The judge continued. "I have also been told that, if at any point you have considered me for a position in the Capital, I should thank you but that my place is in the countryside where I can live my last days in harmony with nature and serve others' needs there."

"As for the matter of the Tribunal," the judge continued, a little hastily so that the King did not try to interrupt and give him a response to what has been said. His ears most likely would not want to hear it. "Regarding the Tribunal, I wish to tell you that it can be interpreted in three different aspects. One can make changes in all three if an improvement is to be achieved." He continued with the following. "Firstly, I want to say that poverty is to be treated not as the lack of something basic from the physical point of view but, rather, from the mental aspect. It had been explained here – and rightly so – that there are people who lack the capacity for producing ideas while others can generate them just fine. Well, those first ones are the ones that end up poor because their mind is not adapted well to live in the times that they happen to live in. It is possible that, if they had been born a few years earlier, they would have been a part of the other group, the one that generates ideas. But now civilization has gotten the better of them, and they do not know how to overcome the mental shortcomings."

"Previously, these people could be helped by them attending the Temple and by those who have an inner voice, but it just so happens that now one has to pay a lot of money to be able to attend the Temple. It should be free, considering the mental benefits that one receives from it. But, as it has been mentioned, this will be discussed on another day."

"It also happens that people who have suffered a misfortune – death of a relative, loss of material goods at an advanced age – by those around them are not viewed for what they are which is ill but, instead, as lazy who do not want to work."

"The mental processes of many people change with the years. It may happen that, people who during their youth were something, later they no longer are."

"Therefore, so that it does not continue like this any longer and that people who are of value do not find themselves in the bad moments of their lives in poverty, it is advisable that all – starting with those who have the most – deposit a certain amount in the treasury of the kingdom. This amount is to be set aside among those who have deposited in their youth. That way, they will have money that they will have deposited themselves when they could afford it. That will, therefore, protect them from possible losses because what they will have deposited will be, by reason, what is returned to them."

"This money can be guarded or loaned out by the Treasurer, but only in the way that ensures that no one who deposited and need it back will have to be told that they have nothing there to give to them. For this reason, they will keep the accounts well maintained. They will keep a record of all receipts and the books where all handovers will be noted."

"One of two things could be done. One, the money is kept in the Treasury, and the accounts are kept accompanied by receipts. Two, a fund is created to be dedicated only to those who now have for when they later do not have. Of course, in both cases, everything ultimately lies with how this will be carried out for, if it is not done properly, it will not be possible to eradicate poverty."

"It will have to be obligatory and done in such a way that no one will receive more than what they have brought in. On the other hand, if the person dies, the money will remain in the treasury. Except if the children or parents of the deceased need it, but the latter will be discretionary for everything will still belong to the legitimate owner if he paid in the deposit himself."

The King liked the theme. And those who foresaw their earnings decrease, after seeing the King's excitement, feigned their agreement.

"Secondly, there are those who have no assets because they have never been salaried. It is obvious that they will never have any money because they spend as much as they receive. When bad times dawn, they cannot cope with their situation and fall into the life of robbery and other outlaw business in order to continue feeding themselves or just to continue surviving. As they have to be provided with a solution too – as they are not prepared for it themselves – the following will have to be done. Naturally, if the King here agrees to it. Whenever they get any paid for work, it will be mandatory that the employer deducts an amount – a small one because they are not paid much – and that amount will be deposited to the Treasury in the name of the person from whom it has been taken. This way, that person will be equal to those who have voluntarily paid in for having possessions. Everything will be put in the same box except that these monies will not be for when they are elderly but, instead, for when they need it or for when they are unable to work. When you work, you save. And these savings will be guarded in the treasury. And, if any worker, through their own initiative, wants to save a larger sum, he can come directly and deposit that amount to be saved for him for the rainy day."

"If someone who has people working for them keeps their money, it will be taken away from them to pay all the workers who the amount corresponds to. And twice as much for the fraud. This falls within the third aspect that I am going to talk about now. So the fine will be twice the size of what has been kept."

They were all taken aback, the King, including. The minister came forward with the intent to intervene and to have some things clarified, but the King cut him off and said:

"We are in the process of Tribunal, and the Judge is speaking. I, myself, have stayed silent when he has referred to me at the beginning. So let's hear what he has to say for, so far, he is doing better than the previous ones."

"There is a third group. This one is made up of people of other races or from other places that come and go because they have nowhere to be or because they suffered misfortunes, such as when an epidemic devastates a Community, or drought, or ice or the wild beasts that killed their livestock. Those people who have to come to the capital – because it is known that poverty in the countryside does not exist – settle for less. Therefore, by lowering the standard and having to help each other, they unite in the Capitals. And so those poor who do not have and those smarts who earn by stealing and exploiting others, all of them form a world that is inconvenient to the Capital."

"First, because they bring diseases. For this reason, what must be done is to maintain a census of the entire population that arrives. As well as of that which resides in the city. Some will have to pay for their wellbeing to form a fund in which money for when they are old or have nowhere to be will be kept. The others will pay from their salaries, and it will be directly deducted by the employers, who will pay it in. And those last ones – who have nothing but who must also be helped – will be supported from the part of the Treasury that will be made up from all the fines paid by those who will have breached the first two points."

"With this money, public dining rooms and bathrooms to rid of the diseases will be sustained. They will also be given clothing in cases where it is necessary. And, of course, there will be places where people can sleep. But, if any of these people can work in order to receive all this, they will have to work for the benefit of the Community. And, if someone does not want to do this – does not want to work for the benefit of others and only wants to be kept by the state – they will be evicted from the city and will not be permitted to return."

"Finally, there are always King's places and farms surrounding the city where lands are cultivated and where the cattle are kept. All this will be worked by those who receive the poverty benefits, and, that way, they will feed themselves, and, among all, it will be of no cost to the King."

123

124

Judge's Dreams I

The Fifth Dream

Three years had passed since the trial of the Gods had been held in the capital. The Chief Judge was leaving his position and retiring, and, before doing so, he wanted to say goodbye to everyone. He gathered all those who had long been suffering under him. Among them was the one who he had left his position as Judge of the capital to, and who would only come to see him once or twice a year, when he had a reason to. He also invited people who remembered him for good reasons.

This judge of the judges also recalled the rural judge who had been a leading figure in some of his great trials, and who he also had significant differences with. He did not want to deprive himself of the pleasure of having the rural judge at this reunion.

The gathering was also to serve as an introduction of the new person who would occupy the judge's position. One would enter, and another would leave, and nothing would stand still; a natural flow that would seem appropriate if it were not for the experience leaving and the youth entering which, you can appreciate yourselves, could be of significant consequence.

The reunion was taking place in the house he had in the country, near the capital, and, although the rural judge took three days to arrive, he did not want to miss this. He had consulted the HIGHEST, of whom he was a servant, in his prayers, asking if he should attend or not, and he had been told not to worry and that all would be fine.

It was known that, sometimes, when someone was leaving the office, they wanted to thank their friends for all the favors that had been shared. But they also wanted to teach a lesson to their enemies so that they would never forget them. The rural judge understood that this man had never respected him and that he was not a good person but, even if it was out of obedience, he agreed to come.

It took him three days to arrive on horseback. The country house was half a distance from the capital, from where he had set off after leaving his Judge's duty. As was said before, he was still called upon. And he was delighted to be able to work a little longer in the post which he had held during the recent years of his life. He will now be able to say that he had experienced and gone through working life.

You see, he had been a soldier first. They had passed through the town where he lived, imposed the obligatory conscription, and took him away. Once he completed the mandatory service and was able to leave, he became a lumberjack. Later, he served as a potter and, finally, a judge. Naturally, the last office was received with the help of the HIGHEST who dictated the judgments, and not for his personal wisdom. Over the years, however, he acquired a lot of wisdom.

When the judge arrived at the country house, he was received by some of the assistants who had already been there for some time. He met some people he did not know but who were also serving in the same office, which he had now abandoned. He presented himself before the master of the house and asked for permission to enter. It was granted without any delay. It was of a great surprise how well he was received.

Once all those who had been invited were in their seats, the principal judge had arranged everything necessary for a good meal to be served. And so the old judge said his goodbyes and, following that, the new judge took office. According to his relative – and in the King's opinion – he was the most suitable for the position. This did not surprise anyone because he himself was a relative of the previous chief judge. It would remain so until someone would bring up the subject of putting a different family in power.

At some point, after the introductions and presentations, it just so happened that the room ran out of subjects to talk about, so someone came up with the idea that it would be convenient to hold one of his famous trials. My father understood that this was predetermined and that this was why he had been invited. He figured that this was a set-up. And that it was done in the way as if to give the impression that the idea came from someone else rather than the principal – the one who was leaving – judge. Everyone agreed that it was a good idea to set up the trial. The subject matter that was suggested was that of the priests.

It just so happened that the predetermined circumstances lead to my father receiving the position of judge. The new chief judge was given the position of a special prosecutor, together with the outgoing chief judge. Thus, everything was arranged in the same way as it had been in previous years. The only difference was that some were no longer there, nothing else.

When the time came, the judge observed that what was missing were the witnesses. So the pair of judges in charge of prosecution went out to look for some neighbors. The defense also went out and found for some servants to act as witnesses. Everything was going smoothly.

At first, as had happened before, the whole process made no sense. But soon, after the new Chief Judge began to give orders and the others started carrying them out, all got organized. Shortly, everyone knew what they had to do and say as the orders had been clear. All were on course in the direction which he had commanded.

The trial began, and the prosecution's argument was about to start when, bypassing the rules, the new chief began to speak first. As a special prosecutor, he should typically wait for his turn, but nobody stopped him, not even the judge. When he finished his speech, the outgoing chief asked for his opinion, and so to a direct question, he replied:

"The chief is making himself known. He needs to be given his time because, for him, this gathering is important. Secondly, the trial process should be changed since the priests are people who obey rules emanating from the Temple. And it does not matter if the companions understand the difference." And with that, he stopped talking.

The old chief realized that the judge was right and decided to set the session straight to prevent it from turning into a work meeting. He ordered his family member to be silent, and so they all began to express their opinions on the matter that they had all chosen: the priests.

In the beginning, they all seemed to be in agreement with the previous arguments that were put forward by the new chief. At those moments, the judge intervened, raising precise and appropriately phrased questions guiding the trial so that everyone could freely contribute their thoughts.

When everything was put in order, the invited judge intervened twice. On one occasion, he had to correct the new chief who displayed great irresponsibility in the process of the trial. The only thing that seemed to concern him was that everyone was clear on who was in charge. So, when the right moment came, he stopped the trial and told him:

"As the trial judge which you have appointed, I must make a case that the argument put forward by the special defense and directed by our chief is not correct in its approach. He does not possess sufficient intelligence to occupy such a high position. Therefore, I revoke it. And I must tell him that everyone has already understood that he is the new chief. But I must also say that, with displays of authority, he speaks nothing more than senseless rhetoric. And that the chiefs must demonstrate greater intelligence and preparation than those who are subordinate." He stopped talking.

He waited for someone to retort, but when the new chief opened his mouth to speak, he did not know what to say. He had expected anything and everything except for someone to put him in his place. He also saw that everyone agreed with the words that were spoken. And, when he was about to get up respond, on his shoulder, he felt a hand. It was the hand of the old chief who got up, thanked for the words, and owned up to them.

The new chief was displeased by this, so he tried to get up again, when he, once more, felt the old chief's hand. He then suddenly realized that the former chief was still in charge and that it would always be so, that he would always be in his shadow until he left this physical world. He did not like the idea and, determined to speak, he shook off the old chief's hand of his shoulder, and got up to speak:

"I want to speak. It is my turn, and I must be respected. And you," addressing the former chief, "do not have the authority to take my position, as I have taken the possession of it now. And you," he looked at the invited judge. "I understand that you feel safe because you are not a judge, and you think you can tell me what you want, but you are wrong. I know that you were mostly right in what you said but not in everything. And about this last thing, I tell you, you are incorrect to try to put me in my place. When this farce is over, and you leave, I do not ever want to see you again." With that, he left. And since it was not his home, a cavalry was heard shortly after.

After this first impression, the trial was concluded, and everyone left the room. All except the rural judge and the former chief who was now deeply concerned. The rural judge, relying on the wisdom that was not his, said:

"I am going to allow myself to give you a bit of advice.

Revoke your relative before the King, explain what happened and how the one who seemed to be a suitable person for the position has proven not to be. You will return to your post, and you should not leave it until the right time comes, and you have found a new candidate."

The former judge thought the idea to be good. He was regretting to have made this decision. Pressure from the family had forced him to do so. And so he asked the rural judge:

"But what arguments do I put in front of the King to explain my mistake?"

The judge said:

"Very simple. Tell him that you are a judge and, as such, you must dictate a judgment based on what was made known to you. And that, if you then learned something new, you must change your judgment. Because you must always seek for truth and justice, and so you hope that this is the best way to serve your King."

The head of the judges excused himself and went to the capital, where he asked for a meeting with the King. The King heard him, but he did not want to back down on something that he only heard a part of. So, when he managed to get out of the judge the story about what had happened, he determined that the trial in the palace would be required and that he would be there to observe how everything developed.

No one liked that. The new chief liked it even less. In a private meeting, he accused the invited judge of insulting him and of verbal abuse, and the old chief was accused of lack of authority and of harming the royal power.

The king, seeing that the situation was taking on a certain appearance, said that everything would be heard in the trial, which would take place in the palace. They were all summoned there, and nobody dared to excuse themselves for the summons was being enforced by armed men.

The judge, as you can all imagine, was as scared as anyone else, but he could do nothing else except for pray and listen to his lord.

His lord, the Highest, replied that he knew what was going to happen, and that he should not worry but, instead, remain calm and speak slowly, and that he would inspire him with words and ideas. This is how it all unraveled.

The trial proceeded with a lot of unease and great caution on the part of everyone. The King, who wanted to stress the relevance and gravity of the matter, determined that everyone considered important, including the ministers, should be present. Thus, from something that was an informal farewell, a great trial was arranged.

To begin with, once everyone was in their posts, the

rural judge asked the King, with the utmost respect, to refrain from intervening. Since everyone, when speaking in the King's presence, would every time wait for his observations, the request shocked them.

When the invited judge spoke these words, a great commotion started, but, rising to his feet, he said:

"By the authority granted to me by the King to preside over this trial, I command everyone present to be silent. And, from now on, each one's behavior is to be appropriate to the place that we are at." They all fell silent, and the trial began.

As usual, the accusations started first, and, as had happened before, the new chief judge wanted to interrupt and be the one to speak because, according to him, he had to be heard first in accordance with the hierarchies' code. Once he finished saying this, the rural judge got up again and said:

"Now that the chief has spoken, and we have all had to keep quiet, the order of justice has been interrupted. With this, an injustice has been committed as, in the eyes of the law, there is no order of importance, and everyone is equal. Only the King can change this, but that would have to be done before starting. And so I order that everything that this man has said is not taken into account and, when his turn comes, he will be allowed to speak. He can then say whatever he deems appropriate."

Everyone remained with their mouths shut because they did not know how the King would react. They were all looking at him, but he seemed to be happy with how events were unfolding and gestured for everything to continue.

As the trial continued, it came out that the priests cared little about the well-being of the people; however, they did care about hoarding money and goods which they did not distribute but, instead, kept in their own the community. It was also said that they had lost Spirituality and that they had become the example of what citizens should not be. They were brutal and callous in their methods, and, of course, few of them were Servants of the Highest. They were only servants of the Temple, which had become a quota of earthly power which should have never been had.

Its influence on the King, on justice, and other powers was significant when, in fact, it should always have been something else entirely.

The accusers did their job well and, once everyone presented their opinions, the turn came to him who had spoken before. He limited himself to saying that he had already put forward all his arguments and that everyone remembered his words that were spoken before the judge interrupted him without giving his words much importance.

When the defenders' turn came, they argued that the priests protected what they had been taught and that the system was the best that can be for the community. They said that, if the clerics dedicated themselves to teaching Spirituality, they would not be able to step back away from the mundane. And so they continued to point out the virtues of those people and their system.

When everyone had spoken, the judge invited the King to say something on the case. The King rejected the offer and limited himself to saying that everything should proceed as usual as he was interested in seeing where it was going to end.

When the judge asked for permission to retire, and the King observed him leave the room, he asked if his needs could not be contained. The former chief of the judges explained that he was a Servant of the Highest and that he never passed a judgment without having prayed first. He explained that he himself verified it and that the judgments he passed were undoubtedly inspired. Apparently, he did not possess the knowledge or wisdom necessary to be able to pass the kind of judgments. The King, somewhat incredulous, said:

"Hang on. I will soon give you a response."

Shortly, the judge came back out. Addressing the King,

he asked for forgiveness for the words that he was about to speak and said that he would never say these things in public but that, given the nature of the trial, he was obliged to convey them. He said that the priests were not the officials of the service of the Temple, just as the Temple did not have to be an extension of the King's power. He also said that the Temple's sole mission was to listen to the HIGHEST and, through him, it could direct, teach, and correct the King and all his citizens.

The King made a gesture indicating that he wanted to intervene, but the judge continued:

"Wait, my Lord. You will see that this does not mean that the King is subservient to the priests; instead, only to the HIGHEST. This is done through those who can reach him and who are purified continuously and remain chaste and pure. These people must stay in places other than the capital. Instead, they would reside in high and well-ventilated places. In places where they can hear their mind's words and elevate their Soul. And the King would come to them for advice when there was something important to consult. Not for everyday or ordinary life business, which he already has his own intelligence and that of others for."

"There is something else I have to say. It is time for the King to correct what he knows because, if this judgment had to be passed, it was not by chance but, instead, because the HIGHEST wanted it. Through the impulses that he puts in people's minds, he wanted this said through one of his servants that is different from those of the Temple who correct the wrong."

"Let him send the priests up to the hill near the capital where they will erect a simple Temple, with decent housing. But not with luxuries. Let them work to construct the building themselves, and that others help them if they want. But that they bend their backs and, this way, purify themselves of the many years that they made others bow their heads in their path."

"Let them shave their heads and go with sandals and a single article of clothing. And let them walk. Since when should priests be allowed to sit on the shoulders of others? Are they lords while the rest are slaves?"

"With respect to you, my Lord, you promote the division between the powers as if in it, your existence lies. But it should be the opposite; we should limit the power of all in the way, which would mean that all depended on you. You in their place."

"On many occasions, the priests and the Temple have caused the King to falter as well as put obstacles in place to ensure that someone who they did not want to be named had not been named. And so it appears that they who should have no other but the Spiritual influence, acquired physical, political, economic, and even military powers for they have guards to protect the Temple and its possessions."

"Lord, all the assets should belong to the King, and should only be used by those indicated. If you assume that it is better to hold Spiritual power than the physical one, surely you will find what to occupy all priests with."

The judge fell silent, and he himself was scared, for he had told the king to eliminate the power of the priests. The same silence was heard emanating from all the others, who were also frightened by the words they heard. They understood that this was the HIGHEST claiming his rights back from his servants.

It was now the King's turn to speak, and so he said:

"I am sure that you have important things that keep you occupied in the village to which you have been retired, but it has been greatly beneficial to meet you. I hope to arrange for another trial soon since I have two to prosecute: one of the military and the other of the judges themselves."

No one liked that, and the King, seeing the faces, laughed out loud. That broke the frostiness in the room, and the Tribunal was over. The King, already relaxed and having a drink, approached the judge to congratulate him, and said:

"I do not know you, and I consider you a dangerous man. But you have been around for a long time, and you have not caused me any harm, so I also deem you to be a friend. Continue in the same way, and we will all be happy."

As for the chief judge, the King approached him and, raising his voice, said:

"I order that the one who held the post and who has done it so well continue to be the Chief Judge. And to the one who had been mistakenly appointed, seek merit so that in the future you can take the post. Because youth does not seem to suit the position."

The man became furious and wanted to protest. However, one signal from the King to the chief of his guard who was already approaching was enough to end the protest before it even came out of his mouth.

The Sixth Dream

The judge, again, felt the symptoms that he usually felt before he was going to dream about a trial at night. He would recant all the details to his wife so as not to lose them as the memory fades, so he could eventually write them down.

The judge could not know what purpose it would serve, for he was a poor, rural judge who had no relevance whatsoever in the social world of today. It could have been because he himself had wanted it that way, or out of obedience, or because the others, in the presence of brilliant men, felt lessened and, because of that, did not want to have any dealings with them; he did not know.

The same thing happened this time. Although, in the previous days, he also felt the same feeling, as if there was something that he had to do that night. And so he stood up, concentrated, said a long prayer, and settled comfortably in his seat.

Within a few minutes, his mental body was traveling to the King's palace. When he arrived, he found the doors closed. He went down to the hall where the meetings take place, learned that no one had arrived yet, and waited. Everything seemed to be set up. Soon, those who prepared the rooms entered. They cleaned the place thoroughly and perfumed the room, spreading the scent of burning trees and leaves.

In a little while, those who were going to participate in the Tribunal that was to take place began to enter. In the previous Tribunal, it had been said that the subject matter would be the responsibilities of the fathers. The last, as it ought to be, the King entered.

The judge had entered a short while before the King did. Whenever the Spirit of the Judge, or the mental body, saw him that looked so much like himself, he felt a slight emotional impression. Partly because everything was a dream and, therefore, in a dream, anything can happen.

Once the formal greetings were said, the trial proceedings were opened. The Minister of Justice was the one to remind that all those present had been pre-warned of the subject matter. As well as of the intention to hear these proceedings in time. Hence, they were expected to come prepared. When he finished speaking, and the King did not seem to want to say anything, the Judge spoke.

The Judge invited the King to introduce the subject matter. The King gladly accepted it and said:

"I think that, in families, many of the problems are the same as those of our society. For example, our young people grow up without principles and our daughters without modesty. If I manage to put in place a Law that would straighten this mess, we will surely all be winners." Seemingly, he had his own problems with two of his sons. His daughter was not old enough yet to bring problems.

The judge understood and asked the others if they had understood the King's proposals. To some, this suggestion that they may not have understood seemed a little insulting, but the judge did not give the floor when they asked for it and continued:

"It is clear that if we want to achieve something new because what we have now does not solve our problem, we are ought to think and present different points of view. Because, if we stick to what we know, we will never get anywhere." While they all agreed, the King had his own mind and said:

"I will not call for any tribunal again. And if I do, I will not start the introduction. Because when I do, this comes, with his own ideas, and changes mine. Although he is right, this does not serve me well in front of my flock."

Various aspects of the allegations were argued. The first one stated that the culprit for the failure of the family was the lack of parental authority. They began by saying that the parent could not use corrective measures on the children, because the children either stormed out of the house or became confrontational. And, since the parents do not have the backing of the Law, they are powerless to discipline those who, from the very beginning, are susceptible to wicked ways. It was said:

"Some of these children that become outlaws are killed or discovered for what they are. Only when this happens that their mothers and families cry, and when they are confronted with, 'What about your responsibility?' they say, 'But they are our children, and we had to protect and defend them.' As if that were so."

"If they, when they first see that things were not turning out well, could teach a good lesson to that who begins to bend and put in place what is necessary, maybe the young tree would then start growing upright."

"Of course," he emphasized again, "that this can only be done if there is a Law that protects them and gives them that authority that they do not currently hold."

"Tell me, which one of you lays a hand on a grown boy, or leaves him locked up, or takes away his freedoms? Because that is when he walks out of the house and goes to live with others. In a place where many of them gather. They end up living without any control, with the worst of the society. And then a daughter goes out, with many desires which she cannot adequately contain, to find herself a man. She ends up sleeping with whoever is the nearest. Then, if she ends up with a child, it is all tears. And she blames the man but not her own choice of life."

The second aspect that was discussed was the local governments of each village. They did not have the necessary conditions to provide everyone with jobs and, that way, to compel all those young people to work. Having nothing to do, they spend most of the day binging, throwing away the fortunes of their fathers. And if they do not have anyone whose wealth they could waste, but they know where they can find some, they end up becoming bandits who rob their own family or close relatives or friends. They know that their misdeeds will be covered up and that they will not have to face the authority. I estimate that, if each place had a competent authority, which would be protected by laws, they could have better provisions when it came to straightening those who were starting to bend before their rehabilitation became impossible.

Then his witness was called to the stand, who put forward a case of the many alleged problems that he had. He spoke about a family with two children. The father, seemingly, did not have enough authority. The son ended up becoming a bandit who wasted the inheritance, got involved in robberies, and left such gambling debts that plunged the father into misery.

The mother, who was in charge of teaching the children, the same as the father, did not know how to do it. She found out that her daughter was sleeping with two or three servants and with her own brother.

When the mother wanted to bring up the subject, she told them both that she had nothing else to do. And that they were to blame for not having taught them well. She also said that she was old enough and that she could have relations with whoever she wanted and that if she wanted to sleep with her father, she would achieve that too. This was precisely what happened in a few days. And this is how it unfolded.

At supper, the father drank a little more than he should have and went to lie down. The mother went out with the animals. The daughter – as the room was dark – went and laid down next to her father. He was a little dizzy and did not realize that he was lying with his daughter. That is how she got what she said she would.

Once she finished with the father, and he fell asleep, she stayed by his side and waited for her mother to return. When she did, the daughter called her to come in. The mother saw them holding each other. Although the man was sleeping, the daughter had put herself under him and had her arms around him. With this, the marriage was over. And, although the man claimed not to remember anything, he took his daughter's side.

That story was so strong that it seemed that they had won in the presentation of their case but, surprisingly, those who were gathered there, sat in silent agreement and shame. Everyone knew of those facts and that those things occurred, but families hid them because these things were shameful. And nothing was done to correct them. Those who had those problems treated them like a skin disease – kept it in a condition that would prevent others from pointing fingers.

The man continued saying that, when the mother reflected upon what had happened and realized that what the daughter had done with her father had been for no other reason but to cause her mother pain, she returned to her husband, and they settled the matter between them. They kicked the daughter out of the house. Soon, the girl ended up in a bad way, and in the hands of those who regarded her as an animal rather than a person.

When the turn of the defender came, he did not have many arguments. He suggested that the education provided to this youth was not adequate and that better options and better outlets needed to be offered to those young people who had problems. He also said that, at the same time, caution should be applied so as not to commit the error of giving all of the attention to the worst and leaving the best behind, because that would cause resentment. He continued saying that he knew of some cases but that they were extreme, and that not everything was bad, and that the society was not so rotten.

After that, his witness gave evidence of how he himself had known of two cases in which the females were starting to turn the wrong way and how the parents, proceeding with a just action and wisdom, had directed them back on the right track. He said that all societies have their moral ups and downs and that, right now, we were living one of those lows.

With this, the morning session was finished. They said their goodbyes and went off to eat before coming back to finish in the afternoon. When everyone left, the King called the judge and said:

"Mind you, I, myself, have children, and they are not without their problems. If you want, when you say your Prayer to help you solve this case, you can consult mine. See, I am not only concerned as a father but also as a King. As you very well know, if the kingdom is not doing things right, the King is the one to suffer the consequences. And I fear that the next King will either die in the wrong hands or he will lead the Kingdom to war and destruction. I have no problems with my daughter. But look into my situation."

The Judge said:

"You see, Lord, this is new to me. I never pray for anything other than his opinion. If he wants to give it to me, he does. If one day he would not, I would not be able to say anything, for I know nothing. But I will ask him, and we will see if he answers. However, do not take this as a negative attitude, only that this is new to me."

The Spirit of the Judge was impressed. While the King was ignorant of the culture, he had a good head and thought not only about the future of himself as a King but also that one of his two children had to die. Note that this was a done thing in those places where there were two heirs.

When one came to power, the other became dead to the brother. What needed to be done was to unify them, and that the two learned the Office together because, if one died – something that did not happen very frequently but certainly was possible – the other was well prepared for the succession.

Some parents, however, maintaining that the position had to be left in the hands of the eldest child, sent the second one abroad. Regardless, the first one would always feel threatened and would continue asking the King where the other child was. The first one would then get the second one killed, and it would be said that he never made it back to the Capital as he had an accident on the road. This would enable him some peace of mind.

The Judge was faced with difficulties because he had to provide two solutions when announcing this coming judgment. He had never handled such a case, except for one occasion. But that was different as one of them was unspecific, and the other had to do with his daughter. Regardless, he retired. Naturally, letting the King pass before him.

In the afternoon, when they met again to hear what the Judge had to say, a particular atmosphere of tension and hope could be felt. Everyone understood that this would be one of the most critical Tribunals that could have taken place, since a possibility existed that, if they came up with something novel, the changes could affect the family life, including their own.

"As you all know, this matter is extremely complicated. So to find a solution that can help rather than leave things the way they always were, we are going to divide the subject into three parts."

"First, parents. In order to be able to raise their children well, they must first know how it is done. Otherwise, they will raise them according to their natural intelligence, which will not differ from how animals do it."

"What happens is that, when they are faced with a new situation, those whose mission is to impose order and good sense do not know what they are doing. This is because they themselves do not practice the order as directed by the mind but, instead, by their habits as that does not require thinking. And, if it happens that they themselves were not taught and that the norms and laws that have to always be minded were not instilled on them when they were young, it leads to certain consequences. They reach adulthood without having known these principles. This, of course, have nothing to do with spiritual principles.

"For this reason, I believe that, if an authority imposed and provided the necessary boost for all young people to go through the Spiritual School, it would expand their knowledge. Not only regarding the energies and the spirit world but would also provide the basic training which would mean that men and women, as they come into adulthood, would know what to do."

Everyone thought it was a good idea, so the Judge continued:

"Of course, this naturally implies that there would have to be more people dedicated to this. As well as that students would not be charged for these teachings as it would be compulsory."

"Since this involves costs, these will be taken out of the taxes that, at the moment, are not being spent because our nation is not in conflict. I remember that when we were last at war, the taxes were raised, and the war was won. Everything returned to normality. The Egyptians are paying high taxes too. Yet, the taxes that were raised during the war have not been lowered. This means that this detail was either forgotten or someone is filling their pockets. And that the reign, of course, wants to have a good reserve in case of another war. However, it is estimated that it has..."

"Young people should not finish their compulsory education at twelve or thirteen years of age but, instead, at fifteen. That is the age when they are already experiencing their internal hormonal developments, sexual impulses, and attraction towards the other. The teachers will be able to teach them to channel these impulses and become experts in this matter. Parents who do not understand these things can leave their children's education to those who do and hold the necessary knowledge."

"But, you see, the other problem is the children. I want to differentiate the two because each one must prepare for what they are going to be when they become an adult. And so they have to continue in this training and education. Those who are going to be merchants will have to train for it, and those who go on to become King's officials will also have to have special education. And here is where the first problem arises. What child knows what training they will need for a particular occupation? And I will give you the job."

"Having gone through the previous training, they will

already be on their way to the next stage. One will be told to go and present himself in a particular place, another one will be told to present himself at an indicated place, and that will be how they learn. Because, see, having children idle in a lazy home and living from their parents, the only thing they will learn is what they see."

"In the case of daughters, who we all know very well will become mothers and wives, their own mothers will be the ones who will teach them from the moment they leave the Spiritual School. They will take them into their care and provide them with the instructions and corrective measures that they will deem appropriate. They will be solely responsible for the future behavior of their daughters."

"In the event of a child turning out crooked, a special process will be put in place. If it is a daughter, she will be put to serve in the field away from the city because, in many cases, the city is where they learn wicked ways. Once she corrected her ways and learned a lesson, she will be able to return home. It has been settled in another judgment – and I recite – that the kingdom will maintain orchards and farms to feed those who have no assets. Thus, they will be considered as those people who need to be looked after. And if a particular case happens, like the one that was mentioned, or if she turns out to be useless, she is removed from the city or sold to a traveling caravan that takes her far from where she can get up to no good because she has the spirit of evil inside her. It is better to have her far away where she will be treated fitting her behavior rather than cause trouble to her family." On this thorny issue, the judge had everyone listening carefully. He continued. "But, you see, these three solutions that have been suggested are for future men and women. Not much can be done about today's men and women except immediately put into action an Authority plan, which will be as follows."

"In a household, a man and a woman rule, and all the others have to obey. If this is achieved, the issue will not have been solved, because the women do not submit to being ruled when they are wives. This is an erroneous way of aligning the authority."

"It has to be set in the following way. In relation to everything that is the outside world, the man commands. In relation to everything that is the homeworld, the woman commands. The man will bring in money as well as means and will be in charge of the provision of goods, and the woman will be in charge of everything related to the administration of the house."

"If someone disrespects these laws, they get expelled from the community. It just so happens that the possibility of being expelled and having nothing to eat creates fear, and, sometimes, this fear of starving or having to work in order to eat will make them conform to authority."

"But you ought to understand," the judge continued. "This is for the now. For later, the essential culture and morals must be instilled through the Spiritual School. The school itself will guide them in which direction they ought to go. They will be taken care of in those places. As for females, mothers will be responsible for them."

"But there are also individual cases," he continued. "One such example is the King's children." He answered the King's private question. And he answered it in public.

"These children have to be raised in a particular way but also go through the Spiritual School. Then, whoever is the heir, will assume the office of arms. Because what is needed is someone who can defend the kingdom."

"But the one who is the second child or any who will not inherit the reign – because it is known that the first one may have a physical or mental defect – will continue their training to follow the Spiritual Office. And it is known that those who serve do not possess pride or appetite for the riches."

"This way, the one who sits on the throne will not have to feel threatened. And not only will he not have to kill the brother but, instead, he will have the other as an advisor, because he will have been taught to think. That way, he will have a Spiritual Master who can hear him out and receive advice from beyond."

"And, lastly," continued the judge, "regarding parents having one or more husbands or one or more wives. It is best that they do not practice this, or they become like animals and, therefore..."

It seemed that the Trial had ended, but then, when all was said, one of the Judges thought to ask if anyone knew how other peoples lived and how they had solved these complex problems. If it is known that others had succeeded in something, one can try and apply the same things here.

That seemed to be a reasonable question. When the Judge spoke, everyone – including the judge himself – realized that some inspiration has come over him, for he did not know these things from within himself, and nor did the others. It was said:

"Two lands border us, one of which, as you all know, is the Egyptian land. We can see what system they have."

"The father is responsible for all and carries great authority. They consider the woman to be an inferior being, let alone a wife. Then, when a man marries her, she receives some of the man's rank and rights. Thus, she becomes the first man after her husband. The rank order is that first goes the first son, then the second son, and so on. Women do not count for anything. They have daughters so that they can be sold or matched, as one can call it. Those who buy them – if they are of equal or of lesser rank – must pay a certain sum. If that who buys her is of higher rank, he who sells must pay the buyer for him to keep her. But they know that the daughter, in the absence of the husband, also acquires the status and power."

"But there was another nation that was spiritually kindred to us. They were called the Semites. Their land, as such, disappeared when the river that bathed their shores dried up. It was a territory of lagoons and rivers, rich with vegetation and animals of all shapes and sizes. Having had that for more than two thousand years, they suddenly found themselves struggling against nature, trying to gradually conquer territories where they could grow grain and feed themselves. It was hard given that before they had the abundance of everything. But the climate changed and, although it did not happen overnight, and it took more than ten or twenty years, we all know what it is like to live in the land without water."

"Well, those people, like us, were dominated by the Atlanteans, whose shackles they threw off using the most ingenious ways one can think of. They utilized young people who had great psychic powers, and who had the ability to detect where the Atlantean ships were. And so they would hide, wait for them, and destroy them."

"One of these young people was made into a Great Master of the Mind. Note that I did not say Spiritual for he was of flesh and bone. And the enhancement of the mind has nothing to do with the spiritual world."

"This Great Master set specific rules which gave his people the inner stability necessary for their growth. This provided his people with peace and a brighter future."

"That great man that the Semites had set very different rules which created a uniformed coexistence. He advocated – and set up – that men and women should be equal, and that they should all have the same rights and obligations. As his people needed to grow in numbers, he ordered that special care should be taken to educate the children. He ordered that it was mandatory for everyone to be educated in order to follow the same culture and, from that, to have equal opportunities. That way, everyone, after having been through three to four years of schooling, would become outstanding at what would serve them well in the future."

"It provided that those who did not comply lost their right to food. And society could not afford the luxury of having bums or bandits. So, instead of having these misfits killed, they would take away their comforts. In those days, it was almost an equivalent to death for surviving on your own was extremely difficult."

"For this reason, he also said that if someone did not want to educate their children in an established way, they had a choice of either changing their way of thinking or leaving the community. They could not have incongruent educators as it would have created continual anxieties in the community and problems for the neighbors."

"When this was ordered, they questioned the chief. They asked, what if the children were all different and each one had their own character? How would a uniformed education fit them all? To that, he said:

'You see, the development of the person means getting each one to achieve the best they can, both in the sense of the mind and the Spirit. And, in that, each one is free. Education sets norms of coexistence among all who live together. And those must be regulated so that no one abuses the goodness of another because he himself is less than good.'

"Everyone seemed to accept it for reasonable, and thus the rules were established.

"Everyone will have to work from the age of four. Children will study, parents will work. If someone does not work, they do not eat. Everyone, once they became of age and had finished their mandatory education, will be taught the vocation that they want to pursue in the future. If they change what they want to be in the future, they will have to go back to education again."

"If one is going to be a farmer, he will have to learn everything about farming. If one is going to become a warrior, he will have to go through weapons training. But if something happens to that farmer or that warrior, or he wants to change his trade himself, he will tell the peoples' elder, and he will see to it that he learns the new vocation."

"If someone wants to get married, they will not be buying or selling or matching. That would be in contradiction with the law. All men and women will be free to find their own partners. But these couples will have to renew their vows every five years. This way, those who are not satisfied in their relationship will separate, and those who want to continue together will be able to do so. But in that period of five years, no one will break up a couple, and no changes within it will take place, as that would break the unity of the family, which is the foundation of our nation."

"If someone, a man or a woman, breaks this bond, they will both be expelled from the community and left to their fate. The change can only take place if both members of the couple give their agreement to the change. That needs to be done in front of the principal. But they will have to wait for the set time to expire."

"If it happens that a girl had a child without a partner, and she did not want to give up who he was, the child gets taken from her, and she gets expelled from the community. If she does tell who the father is and he is single, they will be brought together to raise their child for five years. If they did not want to, their child would be taken from them, and the two of them would be expelled from the community. If the child were from someone who had a partner and if his partner would not be willing to say anything in his favor, they would be expelled for having broken the family bond and for infidelity. The child, in such cases, would always be left in the community because he is not to blame for anything."

"Whenever a disaster would happen, one's children would be raised by others as their own. And if someone did not want to take them in, their own children would be taken from them, and they would be cast out for lack of solidarity. Everyone will treat each other with consciousness and respect. This is how – with rules that were so simple but hard for us to understand – they founded the three great Semitic Kingdoms."

Everyone thought the judge had finished, but then he said:

"And now I shall finish with what I have been told regarding now as well as the future of our people."

"A family unit carries two virtues within it. The father will bear the authority and responsibility of the entire family's economy and everything to do with work outside of the home. The mother will be in charge of everything domestic and inner workings of the house. The children will be the responsibility of both until five years of age. After that age, boys will be the responsibility of the father and girls of the mother. Both until they leave the family home."

"From birth to five years of age, responsibilities will be shared between both parents, and both will carry out common functions since, at that age, there is no need for discipline or remedy."

"The Spiritual Schools will be mandatory to attend between the ages of ten to fourteen and, by the time they leave it, they will be on the right path. The man will be on the path of either a field worker, a merchant, or a warrior. The woman will be a servant of the Temple or a wife."

"If someone violates these norms or there are cases of corruption, special family courts will be set up. These will be responsible for putting everything in order, and the judges will have to undertake specialized training."

"Not only will they have to know all the laws regarding relationships, but they will also have to have a good ground knowledge of the Temple or Spiritual, as well as be a married man. This will give them various perspectives."

"If it happens that one of them has a particular case in their family, a different judge will decide on it. And the same will apply to the King. But, since he cannot be tried, three judges of the highest wisdom will study the case and will give their judgment. The King may choose to have a well-trained advisor, and he will be able to decide whether to follow the judgment or not because he has that power. But the people will provide him with advice on how to resolve his domestic affairs."